SWEET SURPRISES

NICOLE ELLIS

1

"So, you see, if we raise this much money, we'll be able to make a down payment on the old Candle Beach Hotel." Maura Lee held her finger under a line on the Excel spreadsheet she'd printed out to show her budget proposal to the other members of the Candle Beach Historical Society. "We're pretty close to our goal. I think it's doable within the next six months."

Excitement welled up in her chest as she waited for the other women to respond. She'd been in love with the old hotel since the first time another member had shown it to her. There was something enchanting about the grand structure and the grassy knoll it perched on, high above the Pacific Ocean. Unfortunately, the hotel had closed decades before and the building had fallen into disrepair. For years, the historical society had been raising funds to purchase a location to use as a museum and she knew they'd found the perfect place.

"Do you really think that we can afford it?" Gilda Landers asked in a breathy voice. "It's such a beautiful location, but it costs much more than we'd planned on spending." The others leaned forward to review the copies of the spreadsheet that Maura had passed out before her presentation.

Agnes Barnes examined the document with a dubious expression. "That's all fine and good, but how are we going to raise that much money in half of a year? It's taken us five years to get this far in our fundraising."

Maura had known it wasn't going to be easy to persuade everyone that they were ready to buy the hotel, and she'd come prepared. She pasted a smile on her face and faced Agnes. "We've already got the upcoming craft fair at the high school, which usually nets us a few thousand dollars. I was thinking if we hosted some other type of event, we may be able to raise the rest."

She addressed the other half dozen ladies in the small meeting room at the library that still reeked of fried chicken from the Fisherman's Association lunch that had taken place directly before the historical society's scheduled meeting time. "Remember how successful the fundraiser for the Bike Barn was? People were talking about it for months afterward. I bet they'd love to attend something similar for this cause."

"Hmm." Agnes frowned and leaned back in the metal folding chair she'd sat in at the head of the table. "Yes, surprisingly, people did support the Bike Barn fundraiser. But this is another matter. That was to help out a fellow citizen." Her lips curled downward even more. "Everyone around here has allowed the hotel to fall apart for years. As I've said before, I don't think this is the best use of our funds. We need to focus on finding a place for a museum before we lose our storage facility."

"True, but there wasn't much they could do about it before because it's under private ownership." Maura smiled at her again. "And that's where we come in – to remind them how important the hotel is to our town's history. I can't think of a better location for the Candle Beach History Museum."

Millicent Drewes, who was sitting at the far end of the table, cleared her throat. "I think we should put this to a vote. Everyone in favor of Maura's plan to host a fundraiser, raise your hand."

All hands around the table went up, except for Agnes's. She pursed her lips and folded her hands across her chest as she leaned back in her chair. "For the record, I think this will be a lot of work and not much reward. I think we should stay the course and continue our efforts that are already underway."

Maura pointed at the trajectory of a line on her graph. "But we've tried that. At the rate we're currently going, it could take another five years to find a property to use and we don't have that much time. The owner of the location where we keep the collections for a future museum wants to use the space for something else. Besides, I've heard there are developers sniffing around the hotel who want to raze the building and build multistory condos in its place."

"Condos?" Gilda's lips curled down. "In Candle Beach?"

Maura nodded. "I heard it from a friend." She didn't want to say who, in case it was information that her friend Gretchen, a local real estate agent, had let slip accidentally.

Agnes waved her hand in the air. "Ah, the developers have been coming around for years. They're not going to buy it."

"Yeah, but this time the owner has officially put it on the market." Maura let the news sink in, and then said, "Look, I know it's a long shot, but we've come this far and I think we can make this happen."

The women murmured amongst themselves until one spoke up.

"We can't lose the property to a developer," Darla Green said. "We've got to try to save the hotel."

"I agree," Millicent said.

They all stared at Agnes.

"Fine," Agnes said in a tight voice. "We can try Maura's plan. But when it doesn't work, we will continue our other efforts."

The other women became very interested in the spreadsheets in front of them as they fought to avoid eye contact with the formidable Agnes.

Maura took a deep breath and smiled at everyone. "Great. I'll come up with some ideas and bring them to the next meeting."

They closed out the meeting and everyone left. Maura stayed behind to straighten some of the tables in the conference room.

This was going to be a big project, but she'd never been more excited about anything in her life. In her job as a middle-school guidance counselor, she'd met many of the children of Candle Beach and their parents, but even though she'd lived in town for many years, she still didn't feel as though the tight-knit community had fully accepted her.

A love of history had inspired her to join the historical society, and although she was a good thirty years younger than the other members, she'd enjoyed meeting them and feeling more involved in her adopted home town. Besides, it gave her something to do – although she had her job and her crafting hobbies, her social life was sorely lacking.

She moved a stack of chairs over against the wall and eyed the windowless room. It was in high demand with the locals because it was one of the few meeting places in town. Users of the room were supposed to leave it in the same condition as when they'd arrived, and she'd accomplished that.

As she picked up a stray winter scarf someone had left behind, her mind wandered to the Candle Beach Hotel. Owning the hotel would give the historical society a consistent place to meet and they'd even have a kitchen. She was sure that the town would back a fundraiser and they'd be able to continue to afford payments on the hotel using museum entrance fees. Although it wouldn't be their main focus, there was a possibility of occasionally renting out the grounds and some of the rooms in the hotel for parties and other events. It would work. She was sure of it.

She gave the room another once-over and put on her winter coat before entering the main part of the library. After dropping off the scarf in the lost and found and returning the conference room key to the librarian, she exited the library, into the chilly, January afternoon.

It was the time of year where you never knew what type of weather to expect. Luckily for her, it wasn't raining. Her house was only a little over a mile from downtown and she liked to walk as much as possible, especially when she wasn't pressed for time. Being a guidance counselor entailed many hours spent behind a desk, so she got her exercise in whenever she could.

At three in the afternoon on a Saturday, the shops along Main Street were all still open. In front of the bookstore, her friend Dahlia was washing the windows, perched carefully on her tiptoes as her pregnant belly threatened to topple her forward. Maura hurried up to her.

"Do you want me to get the top part of the window?" She nodded at the squeegee Dahlia held.

Dahlia looked at her gratefully. "If you don't mind, I'd appreciate it. I can usually reach it just fine, but this baby is making my balance off."

Maura laughed and slid the tool over the top of the window a few times, then stood back to assess the result. "I think I missed a spot." She swiped at it again, then re-evaluated. "Good."

Dahlia put her hands along the small of her own back and stretched. "No one told me being pregnant would be so miserable. I feel like someone has taken over my body."

"Uh, they kind of have." Maura picked up the cleaning items. "I'll take this into the back room for you, okay?"

"No complaints here." Dahlia followed her to the back of the store, where Maura deposited the supplies.

"Do you want some coffee?" Dahlia asked. "My treat."

"Sure." She didn't have any plans for the rest of the day and could be carefree for the moment. Although she sometimes was lonely, there were advantages to not being in a romantic relationship. She didn't have anyone to answer to for her time.

After Dahlia made the coffee, they settled in two of the comfortable armchairs near the back of the store to drink it. The bookstore wasn't very busy, with only a few people browsing the shelves. Her friend Sarah wasn't working that day and a teenage girl that Maura recognized as a student at the local high school was manning the checkout counter.

Dahlia propped her feet up on the coffee table. "I know they say to enjoy the time I have before the baby comes, but at this point, I can't help but think a baby has to be easier. I'm not looking forward to being pregnant for the first part of summer."

"Are you looking forward to having the baby?" Maura asked. She hadn't been around many babies since she babysat as a teenager, and she was so far away from having children of her own that the idea of having a small person to take care of was foreign to her.

Dahlia sighed. "Yes and no. Garrett is over the moon

excited about the little one coming soon, but I can't help but think of how different our lives will be." She lightly rubbed her stomach and quickly added, "But I am excited too. Just nervous."

"I think that's normal." Maura sipped her coffee, savoring the rich, dark brew, and leaned back in the armchair. The bookstore was pleasantly warm and an afternoon nap was starting to sound good.

"Yeah, I guess." Dahlia didn't sound sure. "Anyway, how are things going with you? I feel like I haven't seen you in a while. Did Sarah say you adopted a dog?"

Maura smiled. "I did. A little Corgi that I named Barker." She grabbed her phone out of her purse, and pulled up a photo of her dog to show Dahlia. "Isn't he cute?"

"He's adorable." Dahlia took the phone to view the photo closer up. "Garrett wants to get a dog, but I think we should wait until after the baby comes. I'm pretty sure we'll have our hands full already." She handed the phone back to Maura. "How are things going?"

"Things are going well. I've been busy with work and some extracurricular clubs I help out with at the school. I feel like I've barely had time to breathe up until the last week or so." She sighed, thinking about everything on her calendar. "Plus, I've been working with the Candle Beach Historical Society."

Dahlia took a sip of coffee, then asked, "Oh really? How is that going? Aunt Ruth used to be a member, but I've never been too into history."

Maura sat up, suddenly energetic. "I love it. Well, some of the members are a bit tough to be around." She held her hand up to shield one side of her mouth and whispered, "Agnes."

Dahlia laughed. "Ah. Agnes Barnes. She's quite a character. But, in all seriousness, her bark is worse than her bite. I suspect that under that facade is a woman who truly cares about this town."

"Maybe. But right now, she's not too happy about my plans to raise money to purchase the Candle Beach Hotel."

Dahlia raised her eyebrows. "The hotel? Isn't that place falling apart? I remember when we were kids, it was rumored to be haunted. One time, someone dared Gretchen to go inside at night." She shook her head. "Maggie and I couldn't believe she did it, but she said it wasn't a big deal."

Maura smiled. "Well, she's been in there now. Her real estate company has the listing for the property. But we'd really like to buy it before some out-of-town developer swoops in and razes it."

"What do you have in mind to raise money for it? What is Agnes so upset about?"

"She doesn't think we can raise the funds to make a down payment on the property, so she's pooh-poohing all of my suggestions." She made eye contact with Dahlia. "I'd love to host a benefit similar to the one held for the Bike Barn's owner."

Dahlia looked at her thoughtfully. "That's not a bad idea. It's been a while since we did anything like that. I'm sure Maggie would offer the use of the Sorensen Farm barn, although it's in high demand now."

"I was kind of hoping she would." Maura blushed. She hadn't been friends with Dahlia and Maggie for long, but she knew they were always up for helping people out.

Dahlia glanced at the register, where her sales assistant was ringing up a short line of customers. A woman stood off to the side, tapping her foot impatiently.

"Looks like someone has a question." Dahlia dropped her feet to the ground with a loud thump. "I'd better get back to work."

Maura stood. "Of course. Thanks for the coffee."

"And thank you for the help with the window. Let me know if you need any assistance getting your fundraiser off the ground. I'm not sure what I can do, but I can always rally Garrett and some of the others to help."

"Thanks." Maura grinned at her. "See you later." Dahlia walked over to help the woman at the counter and Maura left the bookstore.

On her way home, she strolled along the tree-lined streets, enjoying the sound of the birds chirping overhead and the soft breeze that filtered through the barren tree branches. Now that her friend Sarah was happily involved with a man who taught at another local elementary school, she didn't see her much. Thank goodness she'd been introduced to Sarah's group of friends back before Christmas. Without them, she'd probably be going nuts. There were only so many hobbies she could involve herself in before the loneliness set in.

She hadn't dated much since she came to Candle Beach several years ago, and her most successful date was probably the one where Patrick, Sarah's new beau, had professed his love for her friend before they'd even made it to the restaurant. Some may have called it a disastrous first date, but she'd had worse, and at the very least, now she was acquainted with him.

She laughed out loud, startling a squirrel climbing in the tree next to her. If that was her best date in recent years, she really needed to get out more. With the small population of local eligible bachelors though, that probably wasn't going to happen. Maybe Sarah was right and she should go to one of the local speed dating events in Haven Shores, a nearby town. It couldn't be that bad, right?

2

The phone rang next to Aidan O'Connor on the kitchen table, shaking the pile of paid bills that he'd absentmindedly put on top of it. He dug it out and answered.

"Hello?" He held the phone to his ear while continuing to review the document in his hand. His parents had owned many parcels of land in the San Francisco Bay Area, but he didn't recognize this one.

A familiar voice came over the line. "Hi, it's Luke Tisdale."

"Hey, Luke. I haven't heard from you for ages. How are you doing? How do you like it up there in Washington? Is it raining nonstop?" He looked out the window and laughed. "It's gorgeous here. Seventy-two degrees and sunny."

Luke laughed too. "It's not bad. It doesn't rain quite as much here as people say it does. I think they just tell people that to keep the Californians from moving up here."

"That didn't stop you from moving back."

"Hey, I'm a native. They can't keep me out. Speaking of which though, I found something up here that you might be interested in."

"What?" Aidan set the paper on the research pile. He eyed the stacks on the table and groaned inwardly. His parents had been gone for over two years and he felt like he'd never get all of their paperwork sorted out.

"Well, I was remembering how you and Amelia used to talk about using your inheritance to buy a hotel together."

Aidan sighed, then pushed his chair back from the table and walked over to the kitchen window. "Yeah, but that was just a pipe dream. Even if we bought something together, we could never afford a property around here, not with the real estate prices the way they are."

"That's just it. What if it wasn't in the Bay Area?" Luke's voice held a note of excitement that made Aidan pause.

Not in the Bay Area? Although he'd gone to college on the East Coast, he'd never considered living somewhere else permanently. He glanced out the window at the tree house he'd built as a child. When their parents died, both he and his sister were renting apartments in different areas of the city, and they'd chosen to move back into their childhood home together to save money. He'd been working in the hotel industry since he was in high school, and although he'd worked his way up to management, he wasn't bringing home a huge salary.

"I hadn't intended on moving anywhere else," he said slowly. "And I don't think Amelia would go for it. She's been dating some guy here for a while and all of her friends are here." He moved over to the coffeepot on the counter and poured a cup of cold coffee, sniffing it as he tried to remember whether he'd made it that morning or yesterday. "Why do you ask?"

"I think I've found the perfect place for you here in Candle Beach," Luke said triumphantly.

"Up in Washington?" After working in multiple hotels within the city, Aidan wasn't sure what it would be like to own one in a small town on the coast. He shook his head. It was crazy though. Amelia would never want to move, and without her share of the inheritance he could never afford a property on his own, even if it was in a cheaper part of the country.

"Yes, in Washington. I saw the listing for it posted on the window outside my friend's real estate office, and I knew it would be perfect for you and Amelia." Luke sighed. "Look, I know it's not the city, but this place has charm and you can buy it for a song. Candle Beach is a great place to live and you can't beat the coastal scenery."

Aidan considered the idea. His friend seemed excited, and he didn't want to offend him. Even if he was fairly certain this particular property wouldn't work out, it couldn't hurt to find out more.

"Okay, fine. Tell me more. Is it a hotel? How much does it cost?"

"Um, that's the thing. It is a hotel, but it hasn't been in use as one since the early 1980s. It's been sitting there empty."

Aidan's stomach sank. He knew this wouldn't work out. Any building that hadn't been occupied in that long was bound to need extensive work.

Before he could say anything, Luke said in a rush, "Let me send you a photo of it."

Half a minute later, the phone beeped to alert Aidan that he'd received a text message. He clicked on it and an image of a three-story building appeared.

His breath caught. While the hotel itself was badly in need of a coat of paint and who knew what else, the Pacific Ocean was visible in the background and the grounds held promise. At one time, it had been a beautiful hotel.

"Nice, isn't it?" Luke said. "I know it could use work, but it's got good bones."

Aidan continued to stare at the image. Luke was right. It could be magnificent with the right renovation. But what about Amelia? Was there a chance he could afford it on his own?

"Can you send me the listing?" As soon as the words were out of his mouth, he knew he'd committed to the project. If he could make it work, this was where his future lay.

"Sure, I'll find it and send it over as soon as we hang up."

"Great." Aidan paused, suddenly realizing he hadn't asked about what was going on in Luke's life. "How are things going with the barbecue food truck? Is it as popular there as it is here?"

Luke chortled. "Maybe even more so. Seriously, we have tons of tourists and they love the idea of getting food from a truck. I've got a nice setup for my truck here, with picnic tables right outside. It's just off the main street, and on the way to the beach so I get plenty of foot traffic in the summer."

"I'm happy for you." Aidan swallowed a lump in his throat. He and Luke had become buddies when they'd worked out at the same gym. His friend had never truly seemed at peace back then, but he could hear how happy he was now. "It must be nice to be back up there with your grandfather."

"It is." Luke cleared his throat. "And I've met someone here. Well, more like re-met."

"Re-met?"

"She's my best friend's younger sister. I never thought much of her when we were kids, but I suppose we've all changed since then. Charlotte owns a gift shop in Candle Beach that's housed in an old Airstream."

Aidan was beginning to get a mental picture of Candle

Beach. A small town on the coast with plenty of tourist traffic. The perfect place for a hotel.

"I'd love to meet her sometime."

"You should come up and visit. Even if you decide the hotel isn't the right property for you, it would be great to catch up."

Aidan glanced at the paperwork-covered table. It would be good to get away from it all, if only for a little while. At the front of the house, a heavy door slammed shut and footsteps sounded on the entry hall's hardwood floors. A few seconds later, Amelia burst into the kitchen with tears streaming down her cheeks.

Aidan took one look at her and said into the phone, "Sorry, I've got to go. Something just came up here that I need to take care of. Send me the listing and I'll look at it."

"Will do. I hope everything's alright." The phone clicked off.

Aidan set it down on the table and looked up at his sister, who in the short amount of time he'd spent ending his conversation with Luke had grabbed a carton of ice cream out of the freezer and was eating straight out of it with a spoon. Her eyes were still leaking copious amounts of tears. This wasn't good.

"What happened?"

"Darren dumped me." She stabbed her spoon into the ice cream.

"I'm sorry. Do you want me to beat him up?" He joked, but he was only half in jest. Not for the first time that day, he wished that his mother was still alive. She always knew what to say in times like this.

Amelia rolled her eyes and set the empty carton down on the counter. "No."

He motioned to the seat at the table across from him and

she plunked down on a wooden chair that matched the one he was sitting in. "So, what happened?"

"He's moving to Japan for work." Her voice was eerily devoid of emotion. "He said it's a huge promotion."

"You never know," he said, hoping he sounded encouraging. "Long-distance relationships can work sometimes." He wasn't sure he believed that, but it seemed like the thing to say.

"It doesn't matter. He told me that thinking about going there has made him realize that we aren't meant to be together."

Aidan stood from the table and walked over to his sister to wrap his arm around her shoulders. "I'm sorry, sis. He's being a real jerk. I never did like that guy."

"Thanks." She pressed her lips together, as though trying to keep from crying. "Do you ever feel like the world doesn't want you to be happy? Because right now, that's how I feel."

He sighed and grabbed another cup of cold coffee. From the way it burned in his stomach, he was pretty sure it was yesterday's vintage. Right now, though, he didn't feel like being picky. "It only feels that way now. I'm sure things will be better tomorrow."

"Maybe." She dabbed at her eyes with a paper napkin from a basket on the table. "Who were you talking to on the phone when I came in?"

"Oh, that was my friend Luke. Remember we used to hang out when he lived around here?" He welcomed the distance from talking about emotions and being back on solid conversational ground.

She nodded. "Yeah, I think so. Didn't he move away?"

"He moved back home to a small town on the Washington coast." He eyed his phone. Maybe the news about the hotel had come at just the right time. "In fact, he's got a lead on an old hotel for sale in the town he lives in."

It worked. Her eyes lit up. "Can we afford it?"

"I don't know. I haven't seen the listing yet." He checked his e-mail on his phone. "Looks like he sent it. Hold on."

When the listing appeared, he held the phone out between the two of them so they could both make out the information.

After a few minutes, Amelia said, "Well, the price is right, but nothing else seems to be. That place is a dump." She continued to scroll through the pictures the real estate agent had posted.

He had to agree. The picture Luke had sent had been taken at a flattering angle. The listing revealed many more flaws in the structure, include a sagging porch, broken windows, and overgrown grounds. Still though, he couldn't get it out of his mind that this was the perfect property for them to renovate. He scanned Amelia's face, but it was poker straight. It was unlikely that she would agree to purchasing it.

"So? What do you think?"

"I think," she said slowly before a wide smile spread across her face. "I think Mom and Dad would approve. They always did like a challenge."

3

A few weeks later, Maura had worked out most of the details for the fundraiser, but she wanted to take some photos of the Candle Beach Hotel to use in marketing. She drove to the hotel, which was located at the edge of town on a bluff overlooking the ocean. As it had been when she'd visited previously, the grass was long and wild, bending low with every gust of wind.

However, this time, a path of flattened grass leading to the front door of the hotel indicated that someone had been there fairly recently. A rusty NO TRESPASSING sign hung sideways from a thin metal post near the parking lot, but it didn't serve as much of a deterrent. She scanned the outside of the building. The broken windows had been that way every time she'd visited, but there didn't appear to be any fresh damage. Whoever had been trespassing hadn't been a teenager intent on vandalizing the place.

A seagull flew overhead and straight out over the ocean. She followed its path, stopping at the rotting fence that blocked off the edge of the cliff. She couldn't have chosen a better day to visit. The sun reflected off the water and the air carried with it a hint of salt and dried seaweed. Several people were out walking on the beach, and a small child splashed in the shallow water left behind by the receding tide. After filling her lungs with the fresh air, she returned to stand in front of the two-story hotel topped by a cupola with a widow's walk.

When it originally opened, back in the early 1900s, it must have been packed every week during the summer months. She'd heard that people from all around had vacationed in Candle Beach back in those days. Many of them had stayed in town, or returned to build one of the summer homes that marched up the hills that bordered downtown. If the walls of the hotel could talk, she'd bet they had plenty of good stories to tell.

She raised her camera to take a picture of the hotel, making sure to get the ocean in the background. Then she climbed up on the porch to photograph the old barn that stood on the other side of the parking lot. As she snapped a photo of it, out of the corner of her eye, something caught her attention.

Was the hotel's front door ajar? Upon closer examination, she found that the door was cracked open a few inches. Whoever had last been there hadn't made sure to lock up afterward. She looked around the vacant property.

It wouldn't hurt to take a peek inside, right? It had been a few years since she'd been inside with Gilda from the historical society, and on that visit, she hadn't been able to take her time to examine everything that she'd wanted to see.

She tapped the door lightly and it swung open with a loud creaking noise. When she tried to shut the heavy door behind her after she entered the lobby, it bounced open right away. The doorframe appeared to be a little loose – most likely the reason it hadn't been closed in the first place.

The floor inside was dusty, but judging by the footprints,

had recently been walked on. Unease flickered across her mind, but she pushed it away. Her car was the only one in the parking lot, so there wasn't much of a chance that someone else was present. Still, she cocked her head to the side to listen. All she heard was silence in the house and the muted roar of the ocean outside.

Shaking her head, she toured the main floor of the hotel. The first floor contained the kitchen, a small lobby, a great room devoid of furniture but with a bookshelf full of books, a laundry facility and two guest rooms, along with an owner's suite. She knew from the real estate listing that there were twelve more rooms upstairs as well. When in operation, the hotel had provided the area with a good amount of lodging units.

After viewing all of the rooms downstairs, she climbed up the guest staircase that led from the lobby. The window at the top of the stairs was unbroken, but filmy with years of built-up dust. Someone had wiped a small circle in the grime, allowing a glimpse of the beach and ocean.

The first guest room she entered had shards of glass on the floor near the window and signs of water damage from rain blowing into the room. Most of the hardwood floors were still intact though, and while dusty, the beds and dresser looked as they must have the day the hotel shut its doors.

Something skittered near the corner of the room and she froze. A mouse? It wouldn't be too surprising, but she really hoped it wasn't. She'd once lived in a mouse-infested house and had developed a strong dislike for the creatures. She turned in the direction of the noise and breathed a sigh of relief. No mouse. Instead, the culprit was a bedraggled piece of cardboard about a foot square that appeared to have been used to unsuccessfully seal off the broken window.

She moved on to the next few rooms. The hotel was situated so that half of the rooms had a view of the ocean and half of the rooms overlooked the town of Candle Beach in the distance. All of them were fairly similar to the first one she'd checked out. In the center of the long hallway in between the rooms was a small circular staircase. The stairs were dirty, but looked like they'd hold her weight, so she grabbed the peeling wooden railing and went up.

At the top, she came out in a room surrounded by windows that was barely large enough for a small desk and chair. On the other side of the intact glass was the widow's walk she'd seen from outside. This would be the perfect place to watch from safety as winter storms pounded the shoreline.

She wrapped her hand around the brass doorknob of the door leading to the outside, sneezing as her fingers displaced a layer of dust. Before she could turn it to see if the door opened, something clunked from below her. She froze in place, straining to make out the sound.

Another piece of cardboard? No, this was too loud for that. Footsteps came up the stairs from the lobby. This was a person – hopefully the owner of the property. She was again reminded of how isolated she was at the hotel.

"Hello?" a male voice called up the stairs. "Is someone up there?"

There wasn't any use hiding. Her car was in the parking lot, so it was obvious someone was there. Reluctantly, she walked down to the second floor.

A tall, dark-haired man stood at the landing between the first and second floors, where the stairs made a 180-degree turn. He regarded her with a quizzical expression.

"What are you doing in here?" he asked. "How did you get in? I locked the doors when I left."

"Uh, it was open. The door doesn't seem to latch well,"

she added. "But I didn't see any harm in coming in here. The property is for sale and I wasn't going to harm anything."

Why was she explaining herself? She had just as much of a right as him to be there. She straightened her posture and looked directly at him. "What are you doing here?"

He raised his eyebrows, accentuating eyes that were as deep blue as the ocean during a winter storm. "Well, for starters, I own the place."

Now she knew there was something up with him. The hotel was owned by an elderly man who lived in a retirement home in Haven Shores. She didn't think this was a relative as she'd heard the owner didn't have any living kin.

"What do you mean you own the place?"

"I mean I'm in the process of buying it," he said simply.

She stared at him incredulously, ice running through her veins. "You can't be. The Candle Beach Historical Society has plans to buy the property."

He shrugged his broad shoulders. "I don't know anything about that. We made an offer last week and the seller accepted. We close on it in a few weeks, but they said I could come out here before closing to make notes on what needs to be done."

Maura leaned against the wall at the top of the stairs, her vision blurring as she processed what he'd said. Why hadn't anyone told the historical society about an offer on the property? Was this the developer that Gretchen had mentioned? Was he planning on razing the hotel to build condos in its place? Her stomach twisted at the thought of the hotel being demolished. The structure wasn't in great shape, but it deserved to be brought back to life and shared with townspeople and visitors alike.

"Are you okay?" the man asked, as he walked up the stairs toward her. "You look a little ill." He reached out for her. His fingers grazed her skin and she yanked her arm away as if burned.

"I'm sorry." He held up his hands and retreated down a few stairs, but didn't take his gaze off of her. "I didn't mean to do anything to offend you. I just didn't want you to faint or something and fall down the stairs."

"I'm fine," she snapped. Her head was whirling inside. She'd been working all this time to save the hotel. Was it for naught? Was some greedy developer going to win? She'd recently read about some historic buildings in Haven Shores being torn down and it made her ill to think about that happening in Candle Beach.

"Would you like some help out to your car?" he asked. "I think I might have an energy bar in my car if that would help? I haven't had much of a chance to stock up on food here because we're just getting started, but I could get you a water bottle if you're thirsty."

She eyed him. With him standing on a lower stair, they were about at eye level. "I don't need your help." What she needed was to get out of there. She paused, thinking about what he'd just said. Before she could stop herself, she blurted out, "Getting started with what? Planning on what to tear down first?"

She pushed past him on the stairs, throwing him off balance and causing him to grab the railing. Tears were starting to pool in the corners of her eyes. She wasn't usually so emotional, but she'd invested too much time in saving this hotel to lose it now to some outsider. He'd said the sale hadn't closed yet – there had to be something she could do to save the hotel.

"Hey, I never got your name," he called out. He scrambled to catch up to her as she ran down the stairs.

She ignored his statement. He didn't need her name. With any luck, she'd never have to see this jerk again. The front door had come unlatched again, so she pulled on it to open it fully, and walked briskly to her car. She didn't turn to look back at him until the car was in reverse. He stood at the door of the hotel, watching her with his hands over his eyes to block the sun.

4

The woman sped out of the parking lot, the tires of her car sending clouds of dust spiraling into the wind. Aidan leaned against a post on the front porch, trying to make sense of what had just happened. She'd certainly been unhappy upon hearing the news that the hotel had been sold, but it wasn't like he'd ripped the property out from under her. The real estate agent who'd listed it had told him there were other people interested in the property, but no one had made any offers yet.

He glanced at the For Sale sign near the edge of the walkway leading up to the main entrance. He and Amelia had spent the morning at the hotel after they'd gone over some paperwork with Parker, their real estate agent in Candle Beach. When they'd returned, he'd been a little alarmed to find the hotel's front door standing open. He definitely hadn't expected to find a beautiful woman with fiery eyes and a personality to match standing at the top of the stairs to the second floor.

He chuckled. She'd been so mad, but so cute at the same time. Still, it probably wasn't good to have a local upset with them from the start. This project was going to take quite a bit of time and energy to complete and they'd need the town's support to see it through.

"Who was that?" Amelia asked, coming up behind him from the direction of the stairs to the beach. "I was checking out the gazebo and I saw her storm out of here."

He sighed. "I'm not really sure. I found her wandering around inside the hotel. Apparently, she wanted to purchase the property or something. Whatever the case, she's not happy we're here."

"Great. You haven't even been here an hour and you've already caused trouble." She smiled at him to let him know she was kidding.

"Ha-ha. This time it wasn't my fault." His family had always joked that he had a knack for stirring things up. It wasn't his fault that he was interested in people and liked to ask questions – sometimes discovering too much. His love for communication had made him excellent at his job in the hospitality industry, but he may have been better off becoming an investigative reporter. Unfortunately, he hadn't had time to work his magic on the mystery woman or he'd have a lot more answers for Amelia.

"Sure, big brother. I believe you." She grinned and looked at her watch. "We should probably get to work though. I wish we had more time here."

"I know. Me too. But the renters wanted to move in next week, so we have to get all of our stuff out of the house." His heart twinged as he thought about someone else living in their family home. When their parents died, the house had been paid off, so Aidan and Amelia hadn't had to make any decisions about selling the property.

Even now that he and his sister had decided to move to Candle Beach, and they had someone interested in purchasing the house, they hadn't felt comfortable selling their parents' home yet, so they'd opted to lease it to that family for a year. If things didn't work out for them up in Washington, they'd have a place to return to.

He pushed open the front door of the hotel. It squeaked as it swung open, but didn't latch in place when he shut it behind them. The mystery woman must have been telling the truth about the door being open when she'd arrived. He'd have to get a handyman in here ASAP to take care of that so they wouldn't have any more uninvited guests. The two of them paused in the lobby to regroup.

"I thought we'd start downstairs with the Great Room." Amelia glanced at a white legal pad she'd picked up from the front desk. In neat handwriting, she'd listed all of the public rooms in the hotel and what he assumed were their dimensions. "I have some ideas for it, but I wanted to talk to you about them first."

"Sure." He followed her through a narrow hallway to the Great Room.

They'd decided that Amelia would handle most of the cosmetic decorating as she was a talented interior designer, while he would manage the actual renovations. This project was important to him though, and he wanted to have some input into the decor.

She stopped just inside the doorway of the Great Room and swept her hand through the air. "So, I was thinking we could keep the darker parquet floors, but maybe lighten things up with white paneling halfway up the walls and then a lighter paint color above it. Maybe with some pale blue and cream patterned carpets in the seating areas. I'm hoping to echo the tones of the beach and water in here." She glanced over at him. "What do you think?"

He surveyed the room. This was one of the better-preserved rooms in the hotel. For whatever reason, all of the wide panoramic windows with views of the ocean were intact. The parquet floors were scuffed, but should sand down nicely. With white paneling and the natural light coming from the windows, the space would be beautiful.

"I think it sounds great." He had no doubt that Amelia would do a great job. As a child, she'd been fascinated with moving furniture around and decorating her room. It was no surprise that after graduating from college, she'd quickly become a sought-after interior decorator.

"Fantastic." She beamed at him. "I'm going to take more measurements so I can price things out."

He nodded. She left the room and came back with a tape measure, muttering to herself. Her eyes glazed over quickly as she focused on her work. Once she started a task, she kept at it until it was completed, so he took the opportunity to look at some of the books in the library corner of the room.

Thick layers of dust covered the books, which most likely hadn't been disturbed in a few decades. He picked up a leather-bound photo album from the lower shelf and carefully flipped it open on a small table. Musty air puffed out as it opened. Someone had written *Weddings* in careful handwriting on the first page.

He turned to the next page and then to the others. Every page held photos of happy couples in wedding garb. The images looked to date back to the early 1900s when the hotel had opened. Many of them were taken in front of the gazebo and some in what looked like the Great Room. It must have been a popular place for locals to have their weddings back then. With any luck, they'd be able to replicate that popularity when they reopened. He hoped so – they were counting on the place being popular, or they wouldn't be successful.

He flipped to the last page in the book and a loose Polaroid photo with yellow edges fell out. This one appeared newer than the others, and featured a happy couple who appeared to be in their seventies. *Fifty years together and still going strong ~ Darren and Millie Alvins, 1988.* On a hunch, he turned the album back to one of the middle pages. There it was – a smiling couple in their twenties – the Alvins.

He rubbed his thumb thoughtfully over the edge of the newer photograph. Fifty years was a long time. What would it be like to be married to the same woman for that long? He stared at the photograph and a surprising sense of longing came over him. He hadn't had much luck with relationships in the past, but maybe this was a sign that he needed to settle down. The death of his parents when they were just entering their retirement years had taught him that there were no guarantees in life. Each day was a precious gift. A tear pooled in his eye at the thought of his parents, and he blinked it away.

"What is that?" Amelia asked, her tennis shoes squeaking on the wood flooring as she came up behind him. "Is it a book?"

He set the Polaroid photo back in the album and moved away from it so she could view the photo album too. She set her notepad down on the table next to the album.

"Wow. These are beautiful." She carefully turned the pages and pointed at one of the older images with the gazebo in the background. "That's the same gazebo I was in earlier. I wondered if it was original to the hotel or if it had been built later."

He nodded. "This place has so much history. I wonder what we'll find next."

She continued to look through the rest of the photos, then shut it carefully and put it back on a shelf. "I'd like to take copies of some of those photos and display them on one of the walls in here. I bet relatives of some of those couples still live in town and would love to see them too."

"Good idea." He motioned to her notepad. "Did you figure everything out?"

A frown creased her forehead. "Not everything. I need to do some research to find out what type of furniture they had in here. I'd like to replicate some of the feel of the original great room. They must have had more furniture in here than what's left." She gestured at the library shelves and the table they'd used to look at the photo album. "I'm not sure who to ask though since I don't know anyone in town."

"You could maybe start with the Chamber of Commerce? I think they have an office just off Main Street. They'd probably have some idea of who to contact. Maybe someone has kept old photos of the hotel for all these years."

"Good idea." She flipped her notepad to the next page. "Do you want to do the kitchen next?"

He motioned to the door. "Lead the way."

After they'd done a cursory overview of the kitchen together and Amelia had settled in to bury herself in the minute details of the space, he moved outside to assess the exterior. The roof wasn't great and would probably need a full replacement. Many of the windows on the street side of the hotel were broken, although the windows on the ocean side where the Great Room was located had fared better – only one was damaged. He walked gingerly up the stairs to the deck flanking the Great Room.

A gentle breeze sent a leaf dancing across the floor-boards. The salty ocean air and coastal fog had caused the deck boards to rot away in places and the exterior paint on the building's siding to crackle and wear away. This remodel wouldn't be cheap.

Acid churned in his stomach and he reminded himself that they'd budgeted for all of this. An old hotel was bound to have issues, especially one that hadn't been inhabited for close to thirty years. This was a big undertaking though and he wondered, not for the first time, if they were doing the right thing in using almost all of their inheritance to fund the purchase and renovation. If the hotel didn't become profitable within the first two years, they may not be able to make a go of it.

He ran his hand over the rough siding. It would be a shame to not make the hotel come alive again with celebrations like weddings, or full of families on vacation and other travelers in need of the ocean's calming influence. They had to make a go of it, both for the town's sake and for Amelia and him – and for the memory of their parents.

5

Maura drove away from the hotel with her fingers wrapped tightly around the steering wheel, only half-seeing the outline of the familiar road. Usually her emotions stayed pretty even-keeled, but her interaction with the man at the hotel had left her livid. He'd been so condescending to her, offering her food and water, as if he'd already taken control of the hotel and she was a guest there. Her blood pressure rose and her mind raced as she turned off of the highway and onto Main Street.

Why hadn't Gretchen told her that the hotel had been sold, or even that there was someone seriously interested in buying the property? She wasn't sure what she would have done in that case, but it would have been nice to have had some notice, rather than be caught off guard by the new owner.

She and some of her friends, including Gretchen, had arranged to meet for a late lunch at the pizzeria. She'd planned to hang out at the bookstore for an hour or so until Sarah's shift was over, but on a whim, she stopped off at the real estate office to see if Gretchen was there. Although it was a Saturday, when things were busy, her friend often worked over the weekend.

As luck would have it, Gretchen's car was parked outside of the office. Maura tried the door and it opened easily.

"Gretch?" she called out as she walked inside.

Gretchen pulled her attention away from her computer screen, her expression registering surprise. "Hey, I wasn't expecting to see you. I thought everyone was meeting at two o'clock." She eyed her computer and grimaced, then turned her attention back to Maura. "I don't know if I'll be able to make it though. We're slammed with paperwork. Everyone seems to want to buy a house this month." She laughed. "Not that I'm complaining though. Things are going better than Parker and I ever dreamed they would."

"That's actually why I'm here." Maura leaned against the chair on the opposite side of Gretchen's desk.

Gretchen's head shot up. "What do you mean? You're not selling that cute house of yours, are you? Because if you are, I have a client who might be interested."

Maura waved her hands in the air, almost laughing at Gretchen's eagerness. "No, no. It's not my house. It's the Candle Beach Hotel." She took a deep breath. "Why didn't you tell me that someone had bought it?"

"Oh. That. I'm so sorry." Gretchen's eyes were troubled. "I didn't know about it until today when the new buyer came in to sign some papers with Parker. I was going to tell you today at lunch. Things have been so busy around here that I haven't kept up on all of the sales he's been working on as well as my own. I feel bad though. I know how much you wanted that property."

"I did." A rush of sadness came over Maura and the anger she felt for the new owner of the hotel deflated. She pulled out the chair she'd been leaning on and slumped down into it. "It makes me sick to think of someone tearing the old building down. It would have been perfect for the historical society if we could have saved it." Her gaze met Gretchen's. "Is there anything we can do at this point?"

Gretchen shook her head. "I'm sorry, but there really isn't. The only thing that can stop a sale after the offer is signed is if the buyer drops out or the financing doesn't go through."

Maura perked up.

Gretchen held out her hand before Maura could speak. "But the financing is a non-issue in this case as the buyer is paying cash."

"Cash?" Maura whispered. That arrogant man must have been even more wealthy than she'd thought. The price of the hotel was probably pocket change for him in his quest to maximize his investment by tearing it down and filling the space with oceanfront condos.

Gretchen nodded. "Yep. It's a good thing too, because financing may have been tricky given the condition of the property."

"Do you know what he's going to do with the building?" Was there a chance for the hotel to survive?

"I'm sorry. I can't tell you that, even if I knew. Parker didn't say anything to me, but we really need to keep buyer information private. I probably shouldn't have said anything to you about it being a full cash offer."

"Don't worry, I'd never say anything. I appreciate the information though. I guess we'd better start looking for another place for the new museum." She gestured to the front window, which was papered with real estate listings. "Has anything been listed recently that would be suitable for a historical museum?"

"Nope." Gretchen shook her head. "Unfortunately, commercial real estate in Candle Beach doesn't come up all that often in your price range. But if it does, I'll for sure let you know."

"I hope it's fast." Maura frowned. "We're losing our storage rental by the end of the summer and we'll need to move out everything we've obtained for the exhibits. I'd hoped we could move them straight into a permanent museum, rather than try to find a new storage space."

"I don't think it will come to that," Gretchen said. "I'm sure we'll find you something that will work for a museum before then." Her computer made a low pinging noise and she quickly examined something on it, then sighed. "I've got to take care of this right now. I'm not going to make it to lunch though. Please tell the girls I wish I could have been there today and I'll try to join everyone next time there's a get-together."

Maura stood. "I'll tell them – and let me know if you hear anything about the hotel sale falling through."

"I'll be sure to do that." Gretchen smiled at her, then immediately returned her attention to her computer and started pecking away at her keyboard.

Maura left, checking her watch as she stood outside the door. There was still thirty minutes left, so she could hang out at the bookstore until it was time to meet everyone, but some alone time sounded good. She walked across the street to the park to sit on a bench and be alone with her thoughts for a few minutes.

The side of the park away from the playground was quiet, with only the sound of birds chirping in the trees above her and the quiet roar of the ocean in the background. She'd spent most of her free time over the last month planning out a fundraiser for the hotel. Now what? There wasn't much of a point in the fundraiser now that the hotel had been sold. She'd done everything she could, but she'd still failed. Agnes was never going to let her forget that. She drew her knees up to her chest, leaned back against the rough wooden slats of the bench and allowed the sun to kiss her face, giving her some peace.

"Yum. I'm so glad I talked you guys into coming here today. This baby loves pizza." Next to Maura, Dahlia's eyes were as wide as her delighted smile as she dangled a slice of pepperoni pizza in front of her mouth. Strands of cheese hung off the edges, almost reaching the edge of the plate in front of her. She took a huge bite and a blissful expression filled her face.

Sarah chuckled. "I can't believe you've eaten so much."

Dahlia shrugged and rubbed her belly. "I'm eating for two." To prove her point, she grabbed a piece of garlic bread off her plate and chomped down on it.

"Good thing it's a buffet lunch, or you'd be broke." Charlotte tried unsuccessfully to smother a smirk.

"Hey, I'm not even eating for two and I'm happy it's a buffet." Maura grinned and filled her mouth with the Margherita pizza she loved. Pizza had always been one of her favorite foods, ever since she was a little kid. Growing up, Friday nights had always been spent with her parents and little sister, the four of them chowing down on pizza while watching a family movie on the television.

"Stop giving Dahlia a hard time." Maggie sprinkled ranch dressing over her salad. "If I didn't have gestational diabetes, I'd be eating just as much." She grimaced. "I can't wait until I can stop counting carbs."

Dahlia shot her a grateful look. "Only three months left."

"Don't I know it. I'm counting down the days." Maggie laughed and eyed her salad with disdain. "On the plus side,

I've only gained fifteen pounds so far with this pregnancy. With Alex, I think I was already up thirty by this point. It took me years to lose that baby weight. Maybe this is a blessing in disguise after all." As if to prove her point, she stuck her fork in a piece of lettuce and placed it in her mouth.

Sarah smiled and turned to Charlotte. "How are things going with you? It's been a while since I've had a chance to catch up with everyone."

Charlotte's face lit up. "Things are going great. The owner of the new art gallery across the street from my shop wants to show some of my paintings. I think it will be great exposure for my work because most of them are landscapes of the area."

"That's fantastic," Maura said. She'd often wished that she had artistic talent, but her crochet projects were the closest she'd ever get to that.

Sarah leaned over on the bench to wrap her arm around Charlotte's shoulder. "I'm so happy for you. I bet your paintings will sell out almost immediately."

Charlotte beamed at the praise. "I hope so."

"What about you?" Sarah asked Maura. "Even though we work at the same school, I've only caught a glimpse of you from down the hall. We might as well be working in separate cities."

Maura sighed. "The school district decided to have me work part-time at the high school and the other half at the middle school, so I'm over there quite a bit. Besides, you're always busy with Patrick."

"He's been helping me remodel my kitchen, so we've been spending a lot of time together." Her eyes took on a dreamy cast.

"Uh-huh." Maura laughed.

Sarah squirmed and her cheeks reddened. "Okay, okay. I

just love being around him. It's nice to have someone there when I come home from school. I didn't realize before how isolated I was on a daily basis."

"Yeah, tell me about it. I had to adopt a dog because I was so lonely." Maura fought to keep a straight face. She was giving her friend a hard time, but in all honesty, she'd never seen Sarah so happy and was glad that Patrick had come into her life.

"Oh, sorry. I didn't mean..." Sarah's face grew even more red.

"It's okay. I'm totally joking. I haven't had time to be lonely. I've been working with the historical society to buy the old Candle Beach Hotel. That's taken up a huge chunk of my time." She reminded herself again that being single had its benefits, because she had more time to pursue her own interests.

"That's so cool," Sarah said. "I remember my parents saying it was such a shame that it closed down. When they were young, it was a big part of the community. I always wondered why it shut down, but I figured it just got too expensive to maintain."

"Well, they'll be saddened to know that a developer has bought it." Tears came to Maura's eyes at the thought of the beautiful building being demolished.

"Oh, no. I love that place. I've been out there painting several times." Charlotte sighed. "There's something about that spot of land. It's so quiet and peaceful."

"Well, it won't be any more. Not once construction starts." Maura scrunched up her face thinking of how smug the new owner had looked when he told her he'd purchased the hotel. He was more arrogant than anyone she'd ever met.

"Do you know what the new owner has planned?" Dahlia asked. "I may have thought the grounds were creepy when I was young, but I know Aunt Ruth loved the hotel. I hope whoever bought it decides to fix it up."

Maura shook her head. "No, I don't know what he's going to do, but I can guess. I actually met him earlier today. I didn't know yet that the hotel had been sold and I was touring the grounds. He came in and announced that I was trespassing on private property. A total jerk. "

"Ugh. As much as I like the increase in tourist traffic we've had in the last few years, because it benefits my shop, I hate the idea of the old buildings being torn down to make way for progress. The historic buildings are part of what makes Candle Beach so special." Charlotte sipped from her water glass.

"I know. But this guy is from out of town. He doesn't care at all about the hotel, other than using it as a way to make money." A fierce sense of protectiveness came over Maura. "If someone had to buy it other than the historical society, I wish it had been someone from around here."

"I'm sorry about the hotel." Sarah frowned. "That's so disappointing." Her face brightened. "Is there anything we can do? We could go shopping for yarn or something. Maybe a new project would help take your mind off of it."

Maura knew her friend was trying to help, but the passion she'd felt for saving the hotel was vastly different than how she felt about a new crocheting project. Making the hotel into a museum would have benefited the entire town, not just herself.

With a gleam in her eye, Charlotte said, "Or maybe we could find you a date? Luke's friend is going to be moving up here soon. I bet he's single."

Maura groaned. Seriously? Another blind date?

"Nope. No more blind dates." She grinned and eyed Sarah pointedly. Her friend blushed, probably remembering the ill-fated date she'd set up between Maura and

Patrick. "Those never work, or at least not for me. Besides, I don't have time for dating. Now that the historical society doesn't have the hotel property to use as a museum, we've got to find a new location in the next five months, or figure out what to do with everything that we've got in storage. Plus, we're coming up on a busy time of year at the high school with the seniors needing to make decisions about colleges."

"We want you to be happy," Sarah said.

"I *am* happy." It was frustrating that her friends thought her happiness depended on her being in a relationship. She hadn't been in a romantic relationship in many years and somehow, she'd managed to survive.

"She didn't mean it like that," Charlotte said hurriedly. "It's just that we know how hard it is to find a nice guy in Candle Beach, and if you were interested in dating, it never hurts to have friends keeping an eye out for you."

Maura used her fork to trace circles in the marinara sauce on her plate before looking up at them. "I know you're trying to help. If I decide to date, I'll be sure to let you know, okay?"

Sarah smiled. "Good."

"Is Gretchen helping you look for a new property for the museum?" Maggie asked. She'd finished her salad and was now hungrily eying a piece of garlic bread that remained on Charlotte's plate.

"She is, but she's not sure we'll find anything soon. Candle Beach just isn't that big." Maura pushed her plate away. She'd reached the point where she didn't want to think about the historical society or the mess with the hotel for the rest of the day. "I'm going to grab something else from the buffet. Does anyone want anything else?"

"Can you bring me back a piece of dessert pizza?" Dahlia asked.

"Sure." Maura smiled. "Just one?"

Dahlia hesitated, then sighed. "That's probably best. This baby is going to be born addicted to pizza. I should probably eat more healthier stuff." She looked over at a carrot stick lying forlornly on Maggie's plate and wrinkled her nose. "I'll start tomorrow."

Everyone laughed, and Maura got up from the table. She took her time at the buffet, scooping some fruit and cottage cheese onto her plate and placing a slice of dessert pizza onto a separate plate for Dahlia. Back at the booth, everyone was chattering away, smiles lighting up their faces. Contentment eased over Maura. Even though things weren't going her way, she was happy to have such good friends and knew that they'd always be there for her, through both good and bad times. For now, though, she was going to focus on the good. Things would work out with the historical society, and who knew, maybe even with the hotel.

6

Two weeks after he and Amelia flew back to the Bay Area to finish packing up the house, Aidan returned to Candle Beach to start renovations on the hotel. He'd made the drive up Interstate 5 by himself, as Amelia had remained in California to complete a design project she'd been working on for the past few months. A friend of hers had offered her a place to stay as the new renters had already moved into the family home.

Seeing a new family in the home where he'd grown up was bittersweet – while it had been difficult moving all of his parents' belongings into a storage unit, he was excited to start a new chapter in his life. He'd dreamed of having his own place, although the hotel of his dreams hadn't been quite so run down as the one in Candle Beach.

He shut off the car's engine and looked up at the hotel through the windshield. His stomach twisted as he viewed the peeling paint, rotted deck and broken windows. What had he and Amelia gotten themselves into? It was going to take a major investment of time and money to make this place habitable. Had they made a huge mistake? They'd already sunk most of their money into purchasing the hotel. He forced himself to take several deep, calming breaths and exited the car.

Outside, inhaling the fresh ocean air and feeling the warm breeze that rustled the beach grass at the perimeter of the property, he remembered why they'd jumped into the new adventure. Something about the coast was magical, and this place in particular.

At this point though, it didn't really matter whether it had been a good idea or not. He and Amelia had bought a rundown hotel in a small tourist town in Washington state. Only time would tell whether their investment would be a success.

He unlocked the front door of the hotel and opened it, then closed it again to make sure it latched. *Good.* The handyman he'd called had fixed it. He turned the knob again, propped the door open with a large rock he'd found next to the stairs, then returned to his car. After moving all of his belongings into the lobby area, he stopped and stared at the mismatched piles of things.

Although they'd put most of the furnishings from their family home in storage back in San Francisco, he'd brought everything with him that he cared about – which hadn't turned out to be much. A few suitcases full of clothes, some books he loved, a box of photos, and a couple other boxes of miscellaneous items. Not a whole lot for over thirty years of life.

Now though, it was time for lunch. He'd been eager to get to Candle Beach and hadn't eaten anything since the continental breakfast he'd had that morning at the hotel he'd spent the night in. On a whim, he called up his friend Luke to see if he wanted to meet for lunch. The phone rang a bunch of times, then Luke finally answered.

"Hey, buddy," Luke said. "What's up? Are you back in Candle Beach?"

In the background, people were placing lunch orders and asking about the types of barbecue sauce offered. Luke must have placed his hand over the phone's microphone, because he could be heard responding to their questions, but his voice was muffled.

"Hey, I'm sorry. I didn't even think. Of course you're busy now." He wanted to kick himself for bothering his friend. Luke ran a successful BBQ truck in town and this was prime time for the lunch crowd. An unexpected rush of sadness came over him. Until this moment, he hadn't fully realized how quiet the hotel was, especially after the long, lonely drive up from the Bay Area. He'd really hoped to meet his friend for lunch.

Luke said something in the background and then his voice came loudly over the line. "Nope, it's perfect timing. I've been training someone to run the truck on his own, and this will be a good opportunity for him to get some practice in for an hour or two."

"Really? That's great." Aidan's spirits lifted. In the past, he'd been so focused on his career that he hadn't had a lot of time for friends, and he hoped things would be different here. "Where do you want to grab lunch?"

"I was thinking the Bluebonnet Café. It's right there on Main Street."

"I think I remember seeing it," Aidan said. "I'm at the hotel, so I should be able to meet you there in about fifteen minutes."

"See you then." Luke hung up the phone.

Aidan locked the hotel's front door tightly behind him and drove the short distance to town. He parked across the street from the café and crossed at one of the few stop signs in town. Someone, probably the Chamber of Commerce, had hung baskets of flowers from the lamp posts, and the sweet scent of the flowers drifted in the air. This town really was as charming as Luke had promised him.

The café itself was bustling, a good omen for the strength of the tourist trade and the success of his new business venture. When he walked in, Luke was standing at the glass baked goods case, ogling the desserts. Aidan came up behind him and clapped his hand on his back.

Luke turned and reciprocated. "Good to see you, man. Sorry I missed you last time you were in town."

"No problem. I'm glad we were able to meet up now." Aidan glanced around the café. "This place is great. Really, the whole town is great. It's hard to believe that places like this still exist."

Luke beamed. "I knew the hotel would be perfect for you and Amelia. It may not be in the best shape, but it has good bones."

Aidan nodded. "We love it. I'm dreading the repair bill though. Hopefully we'll be able to open at the beginning of summer so we can catch the tourist crowd."

"I hope so too. I grew up nearby and the summer months are crazy around here. The weather is better and we're close enough to Seattle that it's an easy drive for families who want to vacation in the area." Luke signaled to the woman behind the counter that he was ready to order a pastry. He had her box up a large éclair with a half-inch-thick layer of chocolate icing on top.

"Before lunch?" Aidan joked.

Luke eyed the growing crowd. "Hey, if you want something, you have to get it as soon as you see it, or it'll be gone later. These are Charlotte's favorites and I wanted to surprise her when she gets home tonight."

The hostess called Luke's name to seat them before Aidan could ask his friend about the woman he'd mentioned. She led them to a table for two in a back corner of the dining room. Aidan flipped through the menu she'd handed him, but Luke didn't even glance at his.

"People in town will be happy that someone's taken on the hotel. Once you have it up and running, it'll be a great tourist attraction."

Aidan quickly made his selection and set the menu down. "I know one person who isn't too happy we bought the hotel."

Luke raised an eyebrow. "Really? Who?"

"Oh, there was some woman in the hotel when Amelia and I came back from signing the paperwork last time we were here."

"A woman? What did she say?"

"Not much. I got the feeling she wanted to buy the hotel and was upset I was there."

"Weird."

"I know. She just stormed out of there, without even telling me her name."

Luke shrugged. "I guess you're lucky she wasn't there looting the place. Charlotte said that the local teens like to hang out there. I'm sure that whoever it was, she'll get over it when she sees what you're going to do with the hotel."

The waitress hadn't come over to take their order yet and Aidan picked up the menu again, second-guessing his choice. They had a little of everything on the menu, including an assortment of entrées that he was surprised to see offered by a small-town diner.

"Surprised?" Luke asked with a glint in his eyes.

"A little." Aidan pointed at the farm-to-table steak salad. "I wouldn't have expected to see anything like this."

"The owner, Maggie, is a friend of mine. She's big on innovating and is constantly adding new items to the menu. Both the tourists and the locals love it here."

The waitress came over and asked them what they wanted. Luke ordered a hamburger with sweet potato fries, and Aidan settled on a turkey sandwich with fresh cranberry sauce and potato steak fries.

"How is everything going with your food truck?" Aidan asked after they placed their orders. "Is this a new thing, that you have somebody helping you?"

"Yeah, I had somebody in there to help me before, but they didn't last very long. Food service isn't for everybody. For a while, I figured it was easier to just do it all myself. After a few months of that though, the long hours were getting to me, and I wanted to be able to spend more time with Charlotte, so I hired someone new."

"Charlotte's your girlfriend, right?" Aidan asked. "I remember you talking about her when you called me about the hotel, but I didn't get a chance to talk to you much about her."

Luke laughed. "Yes, Charlotte is my girlfriend. She has a knickknack shop a couple of blocks away from my food truck. Actually, that's how we met. Originally, we shared the space.

Well, it's not exactly how we met, but rather how we re-met. Her older brother Parker is my best friend, but we're a couple years older than her so we didn't really hang out together when we were kids." Luke sipped the iced tea that the waitress dropped off for him.

"And Parker is my real estate agent, right? He's Charlotte's brother?" Aidan shook his head. It was like he'd already met half of the town and he hadn't even moved in yet.

"Yes. It's a small town, right?" Luke laughed. "That's what living here is like most of the time. Everyone is connected to everyone else. I have to admit, it's nice after living in a big city. People here really care about each other."

"That's good to hear. I think I'm going to enjoy living here." Living somewhere where people cared about them would be good for Amelia and him. After their parents' deaths, he'd distanced himself from the few friendships he had, and although his sister hadn't been quite so bad with relationships, he'd noticed a change in her as well.

"I'm looking forward to having you here too." Luke examined him thoughtfully. "Charlotte really wanted to meet you. She'll be sad to have missed you again, but she's out with her sister and mother for the day. Something about an annual tea they go to for their mother's birthday. Maybe you could join us for dinner some night?"

"I'd like that." Then Aidan groaned, remembering that he wasn't there for a sightseeing trip. "I'll have to take a raincheck though until after the renovation is done. I have a feeling I'll be pretty busy up to that point."

Luke nodded. "Sure. Let me know though if there's anything I can help with. With our businesses, Charlotte and I know most of the people in town, so if we can smooth any paths for you, we'd love to help."

Aidan chuckled. "Well, if I could get you to sweet-talk that woman I met a few weeks ago, that would be great. I hate to think of someone being so angry that we bought the hotel. But I didn't get her name, so I don't think that's likely."

"It's a small town." Luke smiled at him. "You'd be surprised how often you run into people here – it's like you can't get away from anyone."

"If I do, I'll be sure to let you know." He ate the final fry on his plate and brushed off his hands. "Amelia saw her stalk out of the hotel after talking to me, and I don't think she'll ever let me live it down that I wasn't able to charm her."

"Will do, buddy." Luke took a long swig of iced tea to

wash down his hamburger. "I wouldn't want you to be in trouble with your sister." He flashed Aidan a huge grin.

Aidan just shook his head. It was good to be around friends again, even if he wasn't sure he'd have much time until the hotel opened.

7

Maura's cell phone rang just as she was inserting her key into the lock of her front door. She answered, then propped the phone in between her shoulder and ear and pushed the door open. The force of the inward momentum caused the phone to dislodge and fly onto the rug inside the door.

"Hello? Hello?" cried out a disembodied voice.

Maura sighed and grabbed the phone while eying the pile of grocery sacks that sat outside on the front porch.

"Hello, this is Maura."

"It's Agnes."

Maura held the phone away from her body for a moment to mask the involuntary groan that escaped from her throat. "Hi, Agnes," she said sweetly. "It's nice to hear from you." She reached out to snag two of the bags and slide them inside.

"Yes." Agnes coughed, not bothering to hide the noise. "I need you to do something for the Candle Beach Historical Society."

"Of course." Maura grabbed the other bags and closed the door, carrying one bag into the kitchen while holding the phone to her ear with the other hand. She didn't want to risk dropping it again.

A flash of red and white fur bounced into view through the sheer curtain she'd hung over the full-length window in the back door. A grin spread across her face as she opened the door to let Barker in. He rushed in and circled the kitchen joyously, making her laugh.

"Is everything alright there?" Agnes asked, a touch of irritation in her voice.

Maura returned her attention to the phone. "Yes, sorry, I had to let the dog in."

"*Hmpf*. Anyway, I was supposed to bring some old albums over to the Candle Beach Hotel to show the new owners what it used to look like back in the day. They're quite eager to see them, but I'm not feeling well today." She coughed again.

Maura stared at her phone. "The hotel?"

"Yes, dear," Agnes said as though she were a small child. "The hotel – you know, the one on the water that you wanted to save?"

"I know which hotel you meant." She was trying to keep her words civil and normally she had no problems dealing with Agnes, but any mention of the hotel touched a sore spot now. "Why do you need me to do it?" Why would the new owner care about what the hotel used to look like if he planned to knock it down?

"Most of the other historical society members are busy and there are too many stairs at the hotel for Gilda and Rose to climb up. It'll have to be you."

Maura sighed. She'd rather go to the dentist for a root canal than see the owner of the hotel again.

"I have the albums at my house. I was supposed to bring them to the hotel on Saturday at one o'clock. Please pick them up from my house by this weekend."

"But ..." She searched for an appropriate excuse to not go, but they all seemed flimsy.

"I'll see you soon." Agnes hung up, leaving Maura with her mouth hanging open.

"I guess I'm going to the hotel," she muttered to herself.

Barker nudged her and barked repeatedly. She knelt down to snuggle him, burying her face in his thick fur. He was amazingly good at knowing when she needed cheering up. This winter hadn't been an easy one, but at least she'd gotten one good thing out of it.

Maura gazed up at the Candle Beach Hotel from the parking lot, her mouth hanging open as she tried to process what she was seeing. She hadn't known what to expect – whether demolition would have started already, or if the hotel would look exactly the same as the last time she'd been there.

To her surprise, instead of seeing the building practically crumble in front of her, improvements had been made. She leaned forward for a closer examination. The new owner wasn't tearing the hotel down.

The exterior was under construction, with scaffolding scaling one of the walls. New white cedar shingles had been applied to the siding, and the front door had been painted a hue that matched the dark blue of the ocean during a winter storm, and, if she remembered correctly, the color of the owner's eyes. *Why had she remembered that about him?* She chided herself. She didn't want to be thinking about him at all.

In the few days since she'd received the order from Agnes to be the historical society's liaison, she'd dreaded returning to the hotel and having to see its arrogant owner. Now that she knew he planned to renovate the building rather than demolish it, she didn't know what to think. Although she was happy that the hotel wasn't being torn down, she still had reservations about its future.

She grabbed a canvas sack from the passenger seat, then walked toward the front entrance, her shoes crunching across fresh gravel. She went up the stairs to the wide deck outside of the front door, and rapped on it with the shiny brass knocker. Footsteps sounded across the hardwood floors inside, and the owner appeared at the door. Upon seeing her, he stepped back and his eyes blinked with surprise.

"Uh, hi there. I wasn't expecting to see you again." His words were guarded, as though he expected her to throw eggs at him or something.

She wasn't sure how to take his response. Although she hadn't been very nice to him when she'd seen him last at the hotel, this time she was there in an official capacity.

"Hi." She took a deep breath. "I know I didn't stay long enough to introduce myself when we met before, but I'm Maura Lee. I'm with the Candle Beach Historical Society."

Recognition dawned in his eyes. "I'm sorry, I didn't know that you were part of the historical society." He peered at her. "I appreciate you coming today on such short notice. My sister and I really need your help if we want to do the renovations right." He held out his hand. "I'm Aidan O'Connor."

She shook his hand, surprised by the roughness of his skin. She'd assumed he was management, but he'd evidently been working on some of the projects around the hotel himself. She patted the canvas sack clutched under her arm. "Agnes Barnes said you wanted to see some pictures of what the hotel looked like back in the day. I brought some photo albums from the historical society's collection with me."

He eyed the bag, which was bulging with albums. "Are you sure you brought enough?" He laughed, then held out his arm. "It looks heavy. Can I take it from you? I can't wait to see what you have."

His voice was kind, but she wasn't sure how to respond. Her first impression of him had been that he was an arrogant rich guy, and his pleasant demeanor now was throwing her off guard. And what was that he'd said earlier – was his sister involved in the renovation too?

"I'm fine, thanks." She pressed her lips together tightly.

"Um, okay. Let's get started in the Great Room." He grabbed a hard candy out of a bowl on top of the front desk and held the bowl out to her.

She shook her head. "No thanks."

He shrugged before setting the bowl back on the counter, then unwrapped the candy and popped it into his mouth. "The Great Room is one of our biggest decorating and renovation challenges."

Maura had been in the Great Room before, on the day he'd caught her trespassing in the hotel, and she could see what a difference he'd already made in the room. All of the windows were squeaky clean and the wood trim had been freshly sanded and stained to a dark hue. A faint hint of wood stain hung in the air. The parquet floors had been brought back to their original glory and gleamed in the sunlight streaming through the window panes.

Aidan motioned her over to a pair of folding chairs that were set up alongside a table in the corner of the room that functioned as a library. "We can look at things over here."

Maura pulled out the photo albums, fanning them out on the tabletop, then laid the canvas bag on the floor beside her chair.

"What did you need assistance with?" she asked stiffly.

He sat down in one of the folding chairs, and leaned forward to move one of the albums closer to him. "I was hoping that there would be some photos from the early days of the hotel that would show the type of furniture and decorating used back then. My sister Amelia is my partner in this venture, and she's an interior decorator by trade. She'll have the final say on any of this."

"Oh, will she be joining us today?" Maura glanced back at the door where they'd entered, but didn't see anyone else.

"Unfortunately, she wasn't able to make our meeting today because of something she had to take care of with her previous job." He pulled a small notepad out of his pocket along with a ballpoint pen. "I promised her I'd take copious notes though. I know she wanted to talk with you in person. Maybe we could meet with you again next week?" He looked at her expectantly.

She paused, still trying to wrap her head around what he'd said. He was partnering with his sister on this? When Gretchen had told her that the new investor had paid in cash, she'd assumed that meant that he was part of a larger company. Partnering with his sister was entirely different.

She looked up at him with fresh eyes. "I can probably make room for that in my schedule. I work at the local middle school though, so I'm only available after school or on weekends."

"Really? What you do there?" he asked. "Are you a teacher?"

"I'm a guidance counselor, at both the middle and high schools."

He nodded. "That must keep you busy."

"Most of the time." Why was he asking so many questions about her personal life? And why was she getting so upset about it? She was usually easygoing, but there was something about Aidan that put her on edge. Was it because she'd misjudged him and his intentions for the hotel? She busied herself with the albums, opening the one closest to her and flipping through it in search of images of the Great Room. "I think I saw some pictures in this one that might help." After she'd picked up the albums from Agnes on Thursday night, she'd immersed herself in them. They'd been well kept and provided good documentation of the hotel throughout the years.

Aidan moved closer, looking over her shoulder with his chest almost touching her arm. His breath smelled sweet, like the butterscotch candy he'd just eaten. The close proximity made her skin tingle and she felt her face flush. What was going on?

She reached down, pretending to grab something out of her bag, but used the opportunity to scoot her chair over a few inches to be safely away from him. When she emerged, he'd sat back down in his chair and was lightly tapping the edge of one of the photo albums.

"Please be careful with those," she said. "They're very old and are the only copies we have of some of them."

He smiled at her. "Don't worry, I'm being careful. I wouldn't do anything to hurt them." He pointed at one of the pictures. "These are so cool. Have you looked at them?"

"I've gone through them to see if there was anything useful in them." She leaned in to see what he was pointing at. "Wow. I love the drapes they had in here."

"Amelia will flip when she sees these." He looked up. "Can I keep some of these for her to look at?"

Maura hesitated. Agnes would probably flip herself if she knew Maura had left the photo albums with someone else. Then again, that could be interesting to see. She pressed her lips together tightly to keep herself from grinning at the thought. "Sure. I think that would be okay, as long as you keep them safe."

He snapped his fingers together and jumped up from his chair. "Hey, speaking of photo albums, I thought the historical society might be interested in something I found on the bookshelves." He retrieved a small photo album from a drawer in the table and set it on top of the other albums.

"More photos?" she asked as she reached for it.

"Yes, all of them of the hotel."

She looked through the photos of happy couples, many whom were standing in front of the gazebo at the edge of the property. "Wow. These are great. Do you think we could take copies of them for the historical society's records?" Under her breath, she said, "If only we had a place to display them."

"Excuse me?" he asked. "Did you say something?"

"No." She sighed. It wasn't his fault that they hadn't been able to purchase the hotel property. It had probably been a pipe dream to think they even had a chance of buying it. "I was just thinking about what a great collection we have of photos of the early days in Candle Beach. I would have loved to see it."

"Me too." His eyes glazed over, as if he were imagining it himself.

"Was there anything else you wanted help with?" She stood from the table, clutching the now empty bag.

"Well, if you know of anything else about the hotel, I'd love to hear about it." He frowned. "But maybe that should wait until Amelia is here too. She wouldn't be happy to miss that."

"Okay. In the meantime, I'll try to dig up more information about the hotel to share with you."

"I'd appreciate it. Did you want to see some of the renovations we've done already?"

She hesitated, then scanned his face. He looked so eager to show her around that she couldn't say no. Plus, she didn't hate the idea of spending some more time with him. There was something intriguing about him.

He took her outside and showed her the new deck furniture, siding and paint. "By the time we're done, this place will be brought back to its glory days."

His eyes sparkled as he spoke about the hotel's future and she found herself drawn into them. For a brief moment their eyes locked, then she awkwardly turned away.

"I'd better go if I want to spend some time today in the historical society's archives to see if we have anything else about the hotel." She started walking toward the steps down to the parking lot.

"Thank you, Maura," he called out to her. "It was nice to meet you in better circumstances."

She turned and smiled back at him. "Nice to meet you too."

She got into her car and drove away from the hotel, the short drive home giving her a little time to reflect on their meeting. She'd meant what she said. It had been nice to see him this time and she was looking forward to meeting his sister to see what she was like. It was looking like she'd sorely misjudged him and things were turning out okay for the hotel after all.

8

"Uh, don't we have a meeting with that woman from the Candle Beach Historical Society?" Amelia stared at the boxes of food stacked on the counter of the hotel's front desk.

Aidan's mind raced. Had he gone overboard on lunch?

"Yes. Why?"

Amelia raised her eyebrows. "Because you've got enough food here to feed a small army." She peered at him. "You're nervous about meeting with her, aren't you?"

He shrugged and attempted to look nonchalant.

A wide smile spread across her lips. "You've got a thing for her, don't you?"

His cheeks grew warm at the thought of the enticing vanilla scent Maura wore and how she'd made him feel while looking at the photo albums last weekend. He turned, straightening the food boxes to avoid looking at Amelia.

"Ha! I thought so. My big brother has a crush on a girl," Amelia sang in a high voice as she danced away from him.

He glared at her, but the damage was done. "We have a professional relationship. That's all."

"Uh-huh." She stopped laughing and looked at him.

"You know, you deserve to have a little fun. You haven't been out on a date the entire time we've shared a house. Not since ..."

He knew what she had been about to say. Not since their parents had died. And she was right. He'd been so busy between work and taking care of their parents' affairs that he hadn't had much time for himself. He glanced at the food. Was Amelia right? He felt her eyes on him.

"Don't worry. I won't say anything to her. But the four kinds of fancy desserts might be a bit much." Her eyes twinkled, as though delighted she'd caught him in a weak moment.

He stared at the boxes. He hadn't been sure what Maura would like, so he'd had the woman at the Bluebonnet Café box up an assortment of desserts.

"I can fix this." Amelia winked at him and picked up half of the dessert boxes. She sighed dramatically. "It'll be tough, but I'll make the sacrifice of eating these."

Through the window, they watched a car roll into the parking lot, and Amelia scurried out of the room with the extra boxes.

Aidan took a deep breath and walked slowly toward the door, his heart beating disconcertingly fast. He'd never reacted like this to a woman before. He barely knew her and she was already making him a little crazy.

Maura's steps echoed across the new boards on the front porch, announcing her impending arrival. He glanced behind him to see if Amelia had returned, but seeing that he was alone, he opened the door.

Maura stepped back, as if surprised to see him standing right behind the door. "Oh, hi." She held up a manila file folder. "I did some digging and found some more photos of the Great Room. Maybe they'll help you and your sister with the renovation."

He smiled widely at her. "That's fantastic. I think Amelia has some things to review with you today, and I'd like for you to go through some of the upstairs rooms with me to help me decide which pieces of furniture to keep and which to get rid of. It's not in the budget to get refurbished or replica pieces for everything, but I think we'll be able to find things to give us the atmosphere we're going for."

She nodded and looked pointedly at the lobby behind him. "Is it okay if I come in?"

He laughed nervously and backed up, closing the door behind her after she entered.

She paused in the middle of the floor and pointed at the black and white floral-patterned tiles Amelia had selected. "I like the flooring you installed. I never would have thought to put those tiles in a pattern like that, but they really work well in the space."

"Thanks," Amelia said as she came up behind them. "I found them at a store in Haven Shores, and fell in love with them immediately."

Maura nodded. "Well, they look great." She held out her hand. "You must be Amelia – I'm Maura Lee."

Amelia shook her hand. "Nice to meet you. My brother's been telling me all about you." She turned to wink at him, out of Maura's view.

"Oh, really?" Maura sounded confused.

Aidan held his breath. With Amelia, you never knew what was going to come out of her mouth. He hoped she wouldn't tell Maura that he had a thing for her – that would scare her away for sure.

"He's told me you're quite knowledgeable about Candle Beach's history," Amelia said innocently.

"Oh." Maura nodded. "I've learned a lot about the town since I moved here a few years ago. I hope the photo albums were helpful for you."

"They were. I appreciate you leaving them here for me to look at. Are you ready to get started in the Great Room?" Amelia asked. "I bought a few things to show you, but I'd like to find out if they look like something that would be appropriate to the hotel's early days before I buy more." She laughed. "I may know what looks good in a modern-day living room, but I'm a little out of my element here."

"Sure. I'm ready to get started." Maura followed Amelia into the Great Room, and Aidan trailed behind them. This was really his sister's realm, but he told himself he should stay close in case they needed his opinion on anything.

Amelia led Maura over to a blue velvet sofa that looked like it was straight out of the 1920s. "I found this at a boutique in town. I think it's similar to a sofa I saw in some of the photos you left for us last week." Amelia held the photo album out to her. "I stuck a bookmark in there to flag the page."

Maura opened up the album and flipped to the section in the middle of the book that Amelia had marked. She compared the sofa in front of her with the old photo, before saying, "It's beautiful. It's almost exactly like this one." She ran her hand along the velvety fabric.

Aidan caught himself staring at her and quickly moved his gaze to his sister.

"Oh, good." Amelia's face lit up. "The woman at the store, Wendy, I think her name was, said that it was from the early 1920s. She wasn't sure where it came from originally but she picked it up at a garage sale in Candle Beach a couple of months ago and refurbished it."

"Oh, Wendy's shop." Maura circled the sofa, continuing to run her hands along the smooth surface, as if taking in all of the details.

"Do you know her?" Amelia asked.

Maura smiled. "Yes, she's the mother-in-law of one of my

good friends here."

"She does wonderful work," Amelia said. "I'm surprise I got out of there without buying about five other pieces. I do intend to go back though. There were a few other things that would look great in here, including a credenza for the lobby."

Maura laughed. "I hear that from a lot of people. If my house was any bigger, I'd probably buy something from her for myself too."

Aidan felt as though he were watching a tennis match, with the conversation bouncing between the two women, and didn't feel like he had anything of importance to add. He excused himself by saying that he needed to go check on something in the other room. Thirty minutes later, he was tinkering around with a painted-over window in the kitchen when Amelia called out to him from the doorway.

"We're about done in there." She lowered her voice as she walked past him to pull a pre-made berry smoothie from the refrigerator. "Did you want to invite Maura to lunch? I think she's planning on leaving soon, so now's your chance."

His cheeks warmed. "There's plenty for all of us. Might as well."

She gave him a knowing smile, and they walked back to the Great Room together. Maura was replacing the albums and the manila folder in her bag. She glanced up when they stepped into the room.

"Thanks for having me here. The other members of the historical society and I really appreciate you going to so much trouble to make sure that the hotel is renovated in a fitting manner. It would be horrible to lose this treasure of Candle Beach's history."

"Of course." Aidan smiled at her. "It's important to us too that we get it correct. I've seen some pretty poor remodels of historic hotels and have no intention of making that mistake here."

"I have to admit, I was worried about someone else buying the hotel, but if it couldn't have been the historical society, I'm glad it was you." She frowned. "We still have to figure out a location for our museum though."

"Oh?" Amelia asked. "Aidan had mentioned the historical society wanted the hotel, but I didn't realize it was for a museum."

Maura nodded. "Yeah. We'd been saving up to buy a space for a while and the lease is up on our storage rental at the end of summer, so we need to find a location soon." She looked around the room wistfully. "This would have been so beautiful for it."

"I'm sure something perfect will come up," Amelia said. "I've found things usually work out for the best. In the meantime, if it comes down to it, I bet you could store things here in the barn. I mean, we did buy the hotel out from underneath you, albeit unintentionally."

Maura looked at her. "Thanks. We may take you up on the offer. For now, though, we're going to continue looking for a museum space. You may be right though – maybe the perfect location will come up soon."

"Amelia is right. If you need it, we can probably find some storage space for you here." Aidan gestured to the door leading out to the lobby. "Would you be interested in having lunch with Amelia and me? There's plenty of food. I ordered in from the Bluebonnet Café."

"I don't know …" She looked between him and Amelia. "I really should be getting home because there are some things I need to do before tomorrow."

"Are you sure?" Amelia took a sip of her smoothie. "We'd love for you to stay. Aidan went a little overboard on food and we can't eat it all ourselves."

Aidan glared at Amelia when Maura bent down to pick up a piece of paper she'd dropped on the floor, then busied herself with carefully filing it away in her bag. He held his breath waiting for Maura to respond.

Finally, she said, "I guess I could stay for a little while. I do have to eat, right?"

Aidan felt himself nod vigorously and immediately chided himself. What was wrong with him? This woman had him acting like an idiot.

In a gruff voice, he said, "It's a nice day out. I can bring the food to the porch outside the Great Room if you'd like."

Maura looked out the windows at the Adirondack chairs lining the wide porch overlooking the ocean. "Sounds good."

She and Amelia went outside, and Aidan went back to the kitchen to fetch the lunch items.

When he came back with the food, Amelia popped out of the chair she'd been sitting in. "You know, I totally forgot. I wanted to get a walk in on the beach before it starts to rain."

Maura looked up at the bright blue sky and gave her a questioning look.

Amelia held up her almost empty drink cup. "I'm not really hungry anyway, this smoothie was really filling." Before they could respond, she set her cup down on an end table and scampered down the steps to the lawn. Before disappearing down the trail leading to the beach, she said, "Have fun. Enjoy the food – it looks great."

Aidan laughed nervously as he set the food down on one of the coffee tables they'd set up in front of a grouping of chairs.

Maura's eyes widened as she took in the mound of boxes. "Were you planning on feeding an entire army?"

He shrugged. "I wasn't sure what to get. Plus, there was

so much on the menu that looked good and I had a hard time choosing. Anything that's left over, Amelia and I will live off of for the next couple of days. The kitchen here isn't quite up to preparing full meals yet."

Maura laughed, a happy tinkling sound, and reached for one of the entrée containers to look inside. "Everything I've ever had from the Bluebonnet Café was excellent, so I'm sure I will like any of these." She sat down with the box and opened it wide, revealing a Reuben sandwich, with corned beef piled high on marbled rye. The café had helpfully included a bag of potato chips with the sandwich, along with a pickle and a small bag of baby carrots. She munched on some potato chips, seemingly happy with her choice.

He breathed an inward sigh of relief. He hadn't known what to expect from Maura, but he was happy to see that she was surprisingly easygoing. When he'd first met her, she'd been so worked up that he'd assumed she was normally high-strung.

He chose for himself a clear plastic container containing a fried chicken salad with a side of honey mustard dressing. For a while, they ate without speaking. After a while, the silence was getting to him, so he cleared his throat and set down his fork. "Have you lived in Candle Beach all your life?" He'd caught her comment earlier about moving there a few years ago, but wasn't sure if he'd understood correctly.

She finished the bite of her sandwich. "No, I've only been living in this area for about for five years. I love it here though."

"Oh, really? I'm surprised. You know so much about local history that I assumed you've lived here all of your life."

She laughed. "No, I'm a transplant from the San Francisco Bay Area. I moved up here when I got a job at the middle school after grad school."

He stared at her incredulously. "No way, I'm from the Bay Area too."

She cocked her head to the side. "Really? That's such a coincidence. How did you end up here?"

"It's a funny story. My friend Luke, who used to live near me in San Francisco, had moved back here about a year ago, and he called me up one day to tell me about the hotel property."

"Luke? As in Charlotte's Luke?"

"One and the same." He still couldn't get over the fact that Luke had a serious girlfriend here.

"How did he know about the hotel?" Maura set down her food and gazed at him with curiosity.

He wasn't sure if she was still upset that he and Amelia had purchased the hotel, so he wanted to tread carefully. "He'd seen the listing in the window of Parker and Gretchen's real estate office, and he remembered that Amelia and I were looking for a small hotel to purchase."

"It's a big investment for just the two of you. When I first met you, I assumed you were with an investment firm or something that had provided you with the capital."

"No." A wave of sadness rushed over him. He pressed his lips together as he thought about the source of their money.

She must have noticed his reaction, because her face fell and she quickly added, "I'm sorry. Did I say something wrong?"

He rushed to assure her. "No, no. It's just that ... Amelia and I inherited money when our parents died in a car accident a couple of years ago. Buying a hotel together was something we always talked about doing and it just seemed like the right time now."

"Oh, I'm sorry to hear about your parents. Losing them must have been very difficult for the two of you." She leaned toward him, her face full of concern.

"It was. But I know they would've wanted us to use the money to do something that would make us happy and create a legacy for both them and us." He motioned to the hotel behind him. "This is something that they would have been proud of us for doing."

"I'm sure they would be." Maura took a sip of the bottled water the café had included in the bags of food, then returned to her meal. They ate in silence for a couple more minutes. He felt her watching him before she asked, "Did you grow up in the Bay Area?"

He swallowed and took a swig of his own water before answering. "Yes, we grew up in Canterbury. In fact, we still own our family home there."

"That's such a coincidence. I grew up only about five miles from there." She dabbed her mouth daintily with a napkin. "We used to go there all the time to go to the Canterbury Creamery."

"Really? Amelia and I went there for every birthday and celebration when we were kids."

"I wonder if we ever met each other before this." She shook her head. "And I thought Candle Beach was a small town. It is a very small world indeed."

"No kidding." He munched on his salad and looked surreptitiously at Maura. She was smiling now as she finished her sandwich. He was filled with a happy warmth as they sat there eating companionably. This was going better than he'd imagined. He'd have to remember to thank his sister for leaving the two of them alone to eat lunch together.

With a loud crackling noise, Maura rolled the wrapper for her sandwich into a little ball and stuffed it neatly into the box it had come in. She cleared her throat. "I'd better get going. I really do have some things to take care of before tomorrow."

"Of course." He stood. "Thank you for all of your help and for joining me for lunch. I enjoyed talking with you."

She scanned his face, then smiled. "I had a nice time too. I sometimes get a little homesick, so it was nice talking to someone who grew up in the same area."

"No problem. Anytime you want to talk about home, I'm here." He felt a little stupid saying it, but when he was with Maura, things tended to pop out of his mouth before he could censor them.

"I may take you up on that." She held up her empty container. "Is there a garbage bin where I can put this?"

He waved his hand dismissively. "Don't worry about it. I'll put everything away. I'm sure Amelia will want something when she comes back from her walk anyway." He suddenly remembered the desserts. "Do you want something for dessert? We picked up a selection of things from the café."

She patted her stomach. "No, that sandwich was quite filling. But I hate to pass up a dessert from the Bluebonnet Café – maybe next time."

His heart almost leapt out of his chest. Next time? Thankfully, before he could say something stupid, she set her container back down on the table and started walking in the direction of the stairs to the parking lot.

She turned and waved to him. "I'll see you later. Please say goodbye to Amelia for me. It was nice to finally meet her."

He nodded. "See you."

She got into her car and drove away, this time much more slowly than the first time he'd met her. He watched her until she disappeared from view, then sat back down in his chair, gazing out at the ocean. Candle Beach might be more than he'd bargained for, but he was looking forward to seeing how things went.

9

"Ooh, wait a minute." Sarah jumped up from where she'd been sitting cross-legged in front of the coffee table in her living room. "I have to show you guys what I bought for the babies."

Maura unsuccessfully tried to smother a grin. Sarah was a sucker for babies. Today, Angel, Sarah, Charlotte and Maura had gotten together to plan a joint baby shower for Dahlia and Maggie. Gretchen was supposed to have been there to help them plan, but she was running late. Maura watched with amusement as Sarah ran up the stairs.

"I can't believe two of our friends are having babies in a few months." Angel opened up a notebook she'd brought with her. "It seems like it wasn't that long ago I was trying to convince Maggie that Jake was the right guy for her."

"I know what you mean." Maura leaned back on the comfortable three-seater couch. Although she wanted children someday, having a baby wasn't even on her radar for the near future.

Sarah came bounding down the stairs holding a small box. "I've been dying to show these to someone." She held out two matching onesies. One was yellow, and one was pink. They were hand-painted with an image of a colorful sailboat sailing into a radiant sunset.

Maura reached for the pink onesie. "These are beautiful." She examined the painting on it.

Sarah beamed with delight. "I saw them on one of those online craft marketplaces, and I just had to buy them. They're handmade and remind me so much of Candle Beach."

"They are gorgeous," Angel agreed. "I'm sure Maggie and Dahlia will love them."

"I assume the pink is for Maggie's little girl?" Charlotte asked as she looked at the yellow one.

"Yep." Sarah scrunched up her face. "I wish Dahlia had found out what she's having. I can't stand the suspense."

Maura carefully folded the pink garment and set it on the back of the couch. "I know I couldn't do it. I would want to know the gender as soon as possible."

"Me too." Angel sighed. "I'm happy Maggie is having a little girl though. She said Alex is thrilled to be getting a little sister."

"We'd better get back to planning. When do you think we should have the baby shower?" Charlotte asked.

"I was thinking the beginning of May would work well," Sarah said. "We should be safe enough because their due dates are both about a month away from then."

"Do you think we should do this as a surprise shower?" Maura asked.

Angel laughed. "Maggie isn't big on surprises."

"Dahlia would probably enjoy it, but I have to agree with Angel. Maggie would hate it." Sarah replaced the onesies in the box and set it on an end table.

Maura smiled. She wasn't sure how she felt about surprises either, and she couldn't blame Maggie for not being keen on them. "Okay then. That's one decision we've made." She wrote on her notepad, *Scheduled for early May*.

"Where do you think we should hold it?" Angel asked.

"Ordinarily I would say the Sorensen farm, but it seems a little unfair to make Maggie do some of the work for her own baby shower." Maura tapped her ballpoint pen against her lips.

"We can have it here." Sarah gestured to her living room. "It's not huge, but I think it will be big enough to accommodate all of the guests. My kitchen should be finished by then too." She glanced ruefully at the door at the edge of the living room, beyond which Maura knew was a half-remodeled kitchen.

"Sounds good to me," Maura said. "My place is way too small."

Someone knocked on the door, and Sarah jumped up to open it. Gretchen bustled in and hung her jacket on the coat rack next to the door. "What sounds good?"

"Oh, we decided on a few things for the baby shower. We're going to have it here, and it's definitely not going to be a surprise shower."

Gretchen smirked. "Yeah, Maggie really wouldn't like it if it was a surprise."

"So I've heard," Maura said.

"Did I manage to miss the discussion on the games the guests will play?" Gretchen's eyes twinkled.

Angel patted her on the shoulder. "No, you managed to get here just in time. I remember you mentioning how much you love planning baby shower games."

Gretchen sighed. "Fine, I'll help plan them, but only so I don't get stuck playing the game where we have to taste melted chocolate that looks like baby poop."

Sarah wrinkled her nose. "Yeah, we had that for my sister's first baby shower, and it was disgusting."

They settled on three or four games to play, depending on how much time they had at the shower. After they finished their planning session, Sarah brought out a plate of sugar cookies that she'd frosted green in honor of it being St. Patrick's Day, and a pot of freshly brewed coffee.

"How is it going with the Candle Beach Hotel project?" Charlotte asked. "I heard that they asked you to consult on it for historical accuracy."

Thoughts swirled around Maura's mind. "Um. It's going well. The new owners seem like nice people."

"That's great," Sarah said. "You were so upset about it earlier, so I wasn't sure if things were better now. It sounds like they are going to renovate the hotel properly?"

Maura nodded. "Yes, Aidan, one of the owners, has already taken care of some of the structural renovations. It doesn't look like it's going to fall down any moment now." She thought about the lunch they'd shared, sitting together on Adirondack chairs on the wide porch outside of the Great Room.

It had gone much better than she'd expected and she felt like she had developed a good rapport with Aidan. She blushed thinking about the way his dark eyes had sparkled as he spoke about his plans for the hotel the first time she'd gone over there as the historical society's liaison.

"Aidan is the one I was talking about before. He's a good guy," Charlotte said. "He and Luke were friends when they both lived in the Bay Area."

"He did seem nice," Maura said in a noncommittal manner.

"He's cute too, isn't he?" Charlotte added.

Maura felt everyone's eyes on her face. "I was there for business. I didn't really notice." She felt her words catch as she spoke them and knew that her hesitation wouldn't get past her friends.

"Hey, you like this guy, don't you?" Sarah peered at her.

Maura sighed. "Maybe?" She knew that there was an attraction between her and Aidan, but she still wasn't sure that she trusted his intentions with the hotel.

"What's your reservation?" Angel asked. "You look like you're not sure how you feel about him."

"I guess I'm not." Maura rubbed her fingers against the warm ceramic coffee mug. "He isn't from here, so how can he possibly care enough about the hotel? I know it would have been a stretch for the historical society to have afforded the property, but at least I would've known it was in good hands. What if he sells it to someone else as soon as he's done with the renovations?"

Sarah shook her head. "Maura, I hate to remind you, but you're a transplant to the area too. If you've come to love the hotel as much as you do, maybe Aidan will as well."

"Yeah. That place won't be cheap or easy to renovate," Gretchen said thoughtfully. "Only someone who's truly dedicated to it would put that much effort into it."

"And why else would he have contacted the historical society for assistance if he wasn't interested in preserving the past?" Angel asked as she reached for another cookie. "He didn't have to do that."

Maura pretended to be interested in taking a bite of a frosted sugar cookie, but she could feel her friends' eyes drilling into her face. Had she been wrong about Aidan? They were making good points. Should she give him the benefit of the doubt?

Sarah seemed to take pity on her. "Maybe we should schedule an actual date for the shower today so we can send out invitations soon." She retrieved a colorful striped planner from the dining room. "It looks like we've got Saturday, May eleventh? Does that work for everyone?"

"Ugh." Gretchen frowned. "Parker and I will be away

that weekend at a conference for real estate agents. Would the next Saturday be okay?"

"Neither of them are due until mid-June, so I think it should be fine to have it on the eighteenth," Angel said.

Everyone nodded. Sarah wrote it into her planner and the others made note of it as well. Maura added it to the calendar on her phone that she lived by.

"Do you want me to send out the invitations?" Maura asked. "I saw a cute way of making them online that I think would be fun to try."

"Ooh." Sarah's face lit up. "I'll help. I love craft projects."

Gretchen and Angel both laughed at her enthusiasm.

"You guys are welcome to it," Angel said.

"Gretchen, if you can get Maggie's guest list, I'll talk to Dahlia about hers," Charlotte said, tapping her ballpoint pen against her lips. "Let's aim to get them to Sarah and Maura by next weekend."

Gretchen nodded. "I can do that." She eyed the clock on the wall. "I'm sorry, guys, but I have to get going. I promised Parker I'd check out a new listing with him."

"Don't worry about it," Angel said. "I should probably go too. I wanted to test out a new recipe today for the upcoming chocolate festival."

"Ah, the chocolate festival." A dreamy expression came into Gretchen's eyes. "Parker and I met there."

"Really?" Maura asked. She'd never heard the story before.

"Yep. I think I fell for him the first time I saw him, but our relationship wasn't all sweetness. Some things came between us and I didn't trust him for a while." She smiled. "But that's all old news. I couldn't imagine life without him now."

"You're super sappy," Charlotte said. "But I'm glad you're a member of our family now." She gave Gretchen a quick hug before heading over to the coat rack in the living room. The others followed suit, slipping on their jackets before heading out.

"Thanks for coming, everyone," Sarah said as they walked out the door. She turned to Maura, who was still putting on her coat. "Do you want to work on the invitations after school next week?"

"That should work. I'll find you at school and work out the details. See you."

"Bye." Sarah waved and shut the door.

Maura walked back to her house, enjoying the crisp, clear weather. It would soon be April and the weather would turn rainy, so she wanted to be outside while she had the chance. It gave her time to think too. Gretchen had said that things hadn't always been easy for her and Parker, and now look at them. They were a picture-perfect couple and even worked together. Was it possible that a relationship between her and Aidan could work out too?

10

Maura spent the next morning catching up on household chores – vacuuming the living room, folding laundry and washing dishes. As she set the final dripping plate on the dish rack next to the sink, she glanced out the window. The sun was shining brightly, and although she doubted it was terribly warm outside, she was feeling a little cooped up inside.

She exited the kitchen and called out to Barker, who was curled up on his pet bed in the living room. "Let's go for a walk."

Barker's ears perked up and he trotted over to the door. She put her coat on without zipping it and grabbed his leash, clipping it to his collar as she opened the door. Cold air hit the bare skin on her chest and she quickly zipped her jacket.

They made their way down to Candle Beach's Main Street, occasionally stopping to window shop as they walked down the hill toward the beach. Once they were on the sand, she extended the length of the leash and let him run a bit. He raced ahead of her and she jogged to keep up with him, continually surprised at how fast he could run with his stubby little legs. Every so often, he would stop suddenly to sniff at a piece of driftwood or suspicious patch of sand. She'd never had a dog before and hadn't known what to expect, but he was turning out to be a lot of fun.

Soon the Candle Beach Hotel came into view, perched high above the beach. She reined in Barker's leash and walked toward the hotel. Although she'd seen the building many times, she hadn't paid much attention to how it looked from the beach. From here, the improvements that Aidan had made weren't visible, but it was still beautiful and stately.

She was so intent on checking out the hotel's exterior that she failed to notice Aidan standing near the stairs to the beach until he moved. Barker caught sight of him at the same time and barked loudly in Aidan's direction.

"Shh. It's alright," she whispered loudly. Had Aidan seen her staring at the hotel? She swiveled around and encouraged Barker to run, but instead of moving out of the area, he ran into the nearby seagrass and nosed around in it. She fought to keep the leash from getting entangled in the long green strands of grass, but failed miserably.

While she was working on untangling Barker, she heard someone come up behind her. *Please, please let it not be Aidan.* She cast a glance backward and groaned.

It was embarrassing enough that he'd caught her staring up at the hotel, but she knew he must have also seen her turn away abruptly when she saw him. She tugged on the leash and Barker responded by pushing further into the dunes.

"Hey, I thought that was you down here." Aidan was closer to her, peering into the seagrass. "Is that your dog?"

"Yes." She yanked gently on Barker's leash, but to no avail. All she could see was his stubby tail wagging as he disappeared behind a clump of grass. This was harder than she'd thought it would be. Dog obedience training classes may be needed in the near future.

"Do you need some help getting him out of there?" Aidan shielded his eyes from the sun and looked at her.

Maura stared at Barker. How the little dog had gotten himself so wrapped around everything, she didn't know. Still, he was happy as a clam, spinning his leash in circles.

She sighed. "Yeah, I could probably use some help. I don't have a lot of experience with dogs."

"No problem." Aidan hiked into the grass, and grabbed Barker in his arms. He held on to him tightly as he unclipped the leash. "Try pulling on it now."

To her amazement, the leash slid around some of the biggest clumps of grass, only catching slightly on some particularly thick strands.

With a sigh of relief, she walked over to them and clipped the leash back on Barker, and Aidan set the dog on the ground. "Thanks," she said. "I was wondering how I was going to free him."

Aidan laughed. "We had a corgi like that when I was a kid. Every time we took him to the beach, he'd get into some kind of trouble."

At that moment, Barker lived up to his name and started circling Aidan, barking like a maniac. Aidan deftly stepped out of the noose and Maura pulled Barker away from the seagrass before he could re-enter it.

She gazed at a point far down the beach, hoping Aidan wouldn't say anything about her obvious avoidance of him when he was at the top of the stairs earlier. Luckily, he said nothing about it.

"Hey," he said. "Do you think you might be available to take me on a tour of the area sometime? I've seen most of Candle Beach, but not much of Haven Shores." He drew small circles in the sand with his sneakers while he waited for her response.

Maura clutched Barker's leash against her chest, trying to focus on him wriggling against the end of the leash and not worry about what Aidan had asked her. Was he asking her on a date? Why did he want her to show him around town? She had to admit the idea of spending more time with him was appealing. Although they'd gotten off to a rocky start, she'd enjoyed meeting with him at the hotel last time. They didn't have any other meetings planned, so if she didn't agree to his request, she wasn't sure she'd ever see him again.

"I could do that." She nervously wrapped the leash around her hands, glad of the distraction.

"Great! I'm looking forward to it."

She looked up to see him beaming from ear to ear.

"When would you like to go Haven Shores?" he asked.

She removed her phone from her coat pocket and checked her calendar. "I'm at school all week, but I could do next Saturday."

"That works for me." He was still smiling.

"Okay. I can pick you up around one o'clock. Maybe we can grab a snack in town or something."

"Sounds good to me." He flashed her another smile and nodded at the stairs up to the hotel. "I have contractors here, so I'd better get back to work in case they have any questions. But I'm looking forward to seeing you on Saturday."

She nodded, and he jogged up the stairs to the hotel. When she was sure that he was safely back on the hotel grounds, she walked with Barker a fair bit down the beach and then collapsed against a beach log.

Barker danced around the logs as fast as the thoughts spinning around in her head. This was a date. It had to be. Why else would he have asked her to show him around town when he had other friends like Luke in the area? Her pulse quickened. It had been a while since she'd gone out on a real date.

Her stomach filled with butterflies and she slowed her breath. She'd never been big on dating, preferring to focus on her schooling and career. Oddly enough, back in the fall, Sarah had convinced her to go out on a blind date with her friend Patrick. That date had gone sideways when Patrick professed his love for Sarah, but Maura hadn't been nearly as twisted into pieces prior to that date.

Going out with Patrick had been more of a lark – a date with somebody that she'd never met, and there had been the safety net of knowing Patrick was one of Sarah's friends. With Aidan, it was different. Every time she was around him, the connection between the two of them felt stronger. When she'd first met Patrick, it had been like being with an old friend. Aidan had the possibility of being someone important in her life. She gulped. This was more than she'd bargained for when she agreed to help him with the hotel.

"Barker!" she shouted. The dog turned to listen to her. "Time to run, buddy."

They walked down to the wet grass and jogged back the way they'd come, toward the stairs that led up to Candle Beach's Main Street. When they passed the hotel, she allowed herself the tiniest of glimpses, but Aidan wasn't there. Disappointment echoed through her chest. She'd wanted him to be there, although she wasn't sure how she would have reacted if he had been. She ran faster now, trying to put Aidan out of her head. Her feelings for him were too confusing and she didn't want to deal with them right now.

11

Aidan sat on the top step of the deck outside of the hotel, waiting for Maura to arrive. When she pulled up, she didn't get out of her car right away. Was something wrong? He stood and approached the car. As he drew closer, he could tell she was talking to herself.

He knocked on her window and she jumped slightly in her seat before opening the window.

"You scared me," she said.

"Sorry. I wasn't sure if you were waiting for me, and I didn't want to keep you."

"It's okay. I was just, um, thinking about some things." She gave him a weak smile.

He scanned her face, but didn't want to comment. She obviously didn't want to share whatever it was that she'd been thinking.

She unlocked the doors and motioned for him to get in.

He walked around the front of the car, opened the passenger side door, and slid onto the seat. "I'm glad we were able to do this. I'm excited to see more of the area." He reached behind his right shoulder and pulled at the seat-belt, fastening it securely beside him.

"Sure. I'm glad to do it." She cast a quick glance at him, then looked straight ahead. "Is there anything in particular that you wanted to see? I have a few places I think might be of interest to you, but we can go somewhere else if you had something in mind."

"Actually, there was someplace that I thought would be fun to go to." Luke had told him about a place in town that he was sure would be a fun surprise for Maura.

She turned to eye him. At least he'd finally gotten her attention.

"Oh, really? Where did you want to go?" She tightened her grip on the wheel and looked straight ahead.

She didn't appear to be enjoying the surprise. Should he tell her where they were going?

"It will be better as a surprise." If she didn't like surprises, he was in trouble, but he had a feeling she wouldn't be mad at him when they reached their destination.

She shrugged and started up the car, steering it onto the main highway. "Okay then. But you'd better tell me where we're going, because it won't be long before we're in Haven Shores."

He pulled out his cell phone, and read through a document saved on there. "Looks like we're turning left on Sixth Street, as soon as we get into town."

She gave him a funny look. "Where are we going? As far as I know, there isn't anything out in that area."

"You'll see." He smiled. It was kind of fun to see Maura not so sure of herself.

She took a deep breath. "Okay, but it had better be good."

"It will be."

"Has Amelia been back to finish choosing furniture for the Great Room?" she asked.

"She comes back tomorrow. She should be back in Candle Beach for a while this time. There were a few projects she had to finish up back in the Bay Area, but I think she's almost done with them."

"That's good. It must be frustrating for her to be going back and forth between projects. I'd think it would be difficult to focus." She kept her eyes on the road until they reached Haven Shores. "Is this where we turn?" She pointed at a street up ahead.

"It should be."

She turned onto the street, and he consulted a map. "Okay, it looks like you take the next right here."

They were heading in the direction of the ocean, but past the main tourist areas in town.

"Are we there yet?" she asked.

He just smiled. "Nope. But close."

She kept driving, and soon they were approaching a tall building. This must be the retirement home Luke's grandfather lived in, which meant their destination was very close.

"There." He pointed to the far side of the retirement home.

"Where?" She peered in the direction of where he'd pointed, then dutifully followed his instructions to park the car.

He could understand her confusion. A two-story building stood next to the retirement home. It appeared to cater to the retirement crowd, with a barbershop and hair salon, a small convenience store and an optician's office.

"You'll see."

She exited the car and came around to stand on the sidewalk on his side of the car. He took her hand and she hesitated for a moment, but he held on to it firmly.

"Come on." He couldn't keep the excitement out of his voice. "It's back here."

She allowed him to guide her around the visible stores and office spaces to the back of the building. Just like Luke had told him, there was an ice cream shop on the patio level, with outside seating. A cheery red awning with 'Haven Shores Ice Cream Shoppe' printed on it hung over the door.

Her eyes widened. "It looks a lot like the Canterbury Creamery."

His smile stretched his face so much he thought his skin might crack. He'd been worried, but she seemed really happy about his surprise. "I thought you'd like it. Luke told me about the place. Apparently his grandfather lives in the retirement home next door and raved about it one day. Luke remembered me taking him to Canterbury Creamery one time when we were both back in the Bay Area, so he made sure to tell me about it."

Inside, the floors were black and white checkerboard tile, the chairs were made of black wrought iron with red vinyl padded seats, and the ice cream was kept behind a long glass case in the back of the room. It was the quintessential ice cream parlor.

"My parents used to get us banana splits when we were little at the Canterbury Creamery, but I don't think I can eat a whole one of those now. I really wish I could though." Maura's gaze followed a woman who was walking away from the counter with a giant banana split, piled high with three scoops of ice cream and covered in both hot fudge and caramel sauces. It was topped with a mound of whipped cream and a maraschino cherry.

Aidan's mouth watered, remembering how simply adding ice cream and chocolate sauce to a banana made it taste so decadent. "I was thinking the same thing," he said. "How about we split one?" He nodded at the chalkboard with the flavors on it. "We could each choose a flavor of our own and then decide on one we both want."

"Sounds good." The line moved enough that they could see the ice cream in the vats behind the glass-topped case.

"I think I'm going with the double chocolate brownie," he said. "What about you?"

Maura scanned the other flavors. "Do you want to share the caramel chocolate swirl? That's usually one of my favorite flavor combinations, but something about the raspberry sorbet is calling out to me. I bet they'd be good together."

"Excellent choices." He nodded approvingly. When they were at the front of the line, he placed their order.

A few minutes later, the server slid their banana split across the counter to them. Aidan grabbed it and she picked up some napkins and two spoons. Together, they edged their way out of the crowds and through the door.

When they were free of the ice cream shop, he held up the sundae for her to see, laughing at how much her eyes bugged out.

"Good thing I had a salad for lunch," she joked.

"I didn't, but I think I can make room." He rubbed his stomach with his free hand, while carefully balancing the banana split in the palm of his other hand.

She looked around at the full tables on the patio. "Where did all these people come from? I don't think there's anywhere to sit."

He shrugged. "Yeah, no kidding. It's like someone dropped off a tourist bus full of people or something." He doubted that was the case, but she was right – there were at least twenty more people there than when they'd arrived. Whatever the reason, there weren't any seats left. "Do you want to take it out on the beach to eat?"

"Sure." She laughed. "As a bonus, if we spill, we won't have to clean it up." She followed him onto to the beach. He noticed she kept sneaking hungry looks at the sundae the whole time. As soon as they reached the sand, she used one of the spoons and picked up a scoopful of raspberry sorbet with chocolate sauce.

A look of joy came over her face as her lips closed around the spoon. "This is amazing!"

"I hear they make their own hot fudge and caramel sauces, just like Canterbury Creamery." He took a bite of the double fudge brownie ice cream he'd selected and his eyes practically rolled back in his head. "Yep, that's homemade hot fudge."

They walked over to a log on the beach and sat down to consume the rest of the sundae. After they took turns scraping the bottom of the plastic dish, he handed her a napkin.

"You've got a little ice cream on your cheek."

"I do?" Her eyes grew big as she dabbed at her face. "Where?"

He reached over and wiped off the smudge with his finger. Her skin was soft and smooth and he allowed his finger to linger a little longer than necessary.

She smiled at him, as if she knew too. "Thanks," she said softly. "Taking me there was one of the nicest things anyone's ever done for me. I've been missing home lately and it was nice to take that trip down memory lane."

"Of course," he said. "What did you think? Was this worth waiting for the surprise?"

She nodded her head vigorously. "I loved it."

"I thought you weren't going to make it. You seemed like you were getting upset when we were driving there. I was getting worried you were mad at me."

She sighed. "I tend to get a little crazy when I'm not in control of a situation. But I think it's good for me to let go sometimes."

"Good to know." He smiled at her. "Maybe I can come up with another surprise for you sometime."

She cocked her head to the side. "Do you still want to see more of Haven Shores, or was that a cleverly disguised reason to go out with me?" Her eyes twinkled as she spoke.

"You got me." He grinned. He loved the way her nose crinkled up when she asked a question. "But I wouldn't mind a tour of town. I really would like to see the area."

"Okay." She hopped off of the log, onto the sand. "Let's go. After that sundae, I'm not really hungry, but there's a Thai restaurant in town that I love. Maybe by the time we drive around for a while, I'll be ready to eat again. Ooh. We could go to the history museum here. I've been there before, but I'd love to check it out again."

"Sounds exciting." He wouldn't normally think of a history museum as a prime date location, but he had a feeling Maura's enthusiasm for the subject would shine through and he'd be pleasantly surprised.

They toured the museum and the rest of town, then had dinner at the Thai restaurant she'd mentioned. When they arrived back at the Candle Beach Hotel, the sky was dark, but after the fun they'd had, he didn't want their date to end.

"Would you like to see the turret at the top of the hotel? We just finished it and the widow's walk this past week." He looked over at her hopefully.

She gazed up at the third floor of the hotel. "Sure. I'd love to see it again." She eyed him pointedly. "Last time I was there, I didn't get to finish seeing it because someone called me down before I could go outside."

He laughed. "Sorry about that. I didn't know if you were a vandal or something. All I knew was that someone was in the hotel and I didn't know who." He hopped out of the car and came around to her side, opening the door for her.

"Thanks." She flashed him a smile, then took the arm he offered. "Is Amelia in town?"

"She went to Seattle for the day to pick up some furnishings." He checked his watch. "I think she'll be back in a few hours. Why, do you think we need a chaperone?" He paused, hoping she knew he was teasing.

"I don't know, what do you have planned?" She mock-glared at him. "Wait, was this all part of the plan? To get me out here alone?"

"No, no." He didn't want her to think that. "I honestly thought it would be nice to go up in the turret tonight. It's such a clear night." He stopped and examined her face. She was smiling up at him – she wasn't upset. He breathed a sigh of relief.

"I think you're right. It is a perfect night to view the stars." She followed him into the hotel and up the winding staircase to the turret, stopping in front of the windows. "Oh, wow."

"Beautiful, right?" He came behind her and reached forward to open the door to the widow's walk. They moved outside, standing together at the railing. It was chilly in the night air, but worth it.

The stars shone brightly overhead, and the moon glinted off the ocean, casting silvery strands of light on the tips of the waves. Except for the sound of the surf, the air was quiet.

"I feel like I'm in some other world," Maura whispered. "It's so gorgeous."

"It is. We ended up having to replace all of the floorboards up here and install new windows, which was costly, but I think it was well worth it." He edged closer to her and put a tentative arm around her shoulder. She snuggled into him, and he slid his hand down her arm to rest at her waist. She sighed happily and turned into him until both his hands were on her waist and she was gazing up at his face.

"I had a really nice time with you today." She rested her hands on his arms.

"Me too." He brushed some strands of hair away from her face and his eyes met hers. She stretched upward and closed her eyes, which he took as his cue, leaning down to kiss her lips. They were soft and warm, and felt even better than he'd imagined they would.

Her heels settled on the ground, breaking their physical connection, but she continued to look into his eyes, with her arms wrapped firmly around his neck. Suddenly, she laughed, and he stepped back.

"What? Did I do something wrong?"

"No, no." She laughed again. "It's just that a few weeks ago, I hated you and wanted nothing more than to never see you again. Now I can hardly imagine thinking that. Aidan O'Connor, you are full of surprises."

He smiled. "You haven't seen anything yet."

He kissed her again, happy that she'd given him the opportunity to change her mind about him. From the moment he'd first met her, he'd been intrigued, but now he was captivated by this woman. The hotel renovation may not have been going completely according to plan, but his new relationship with Maura was more than making up for it.

12

"So, who is going to be at game night?" Aidan stopped on the sidewalk, still holding on to Maura's hand.

She smiled. He was more nervous about officially meeting her friends than she'd expected. They'd been dating for a couple of weeks, but things had been so busy that she hadn't had a chance to introduce him to them yet.

"My friend from school, Sarah, and her boyfriend, Patrick. Her brother, Adam, and his girlfriend, Angel. And of course, you already know Luke and Charlotte." She squeezed his hand. "Don't worry. They'll love you."

He gave her a feeble smile. "I'm not used to meeting so many new people – or having time to hang out with friends."

"What about back in San Francisco? You must have met people all the time at the hotel." She looked up at him with curiosity. Aidan was one of the most outgoing people she'd ever met, so this sudden shyness was actually fairly amusing.

"It's different. Any relationships I had with guests at the hotel were superficial, even with people who came to stay there regularly. As much as I loved meeting them, I was there to make their stay better, not to be friends with them." He guided her around a tree that jutted out over the sidewalk. "I was so busy though, that I rarely had time for friends. Luke and I met at the gym and our friendship consisted of saying hi to each other there and occasionally grabbing a beer and pizza afterward." He laughed. "Probably not the healthiest thing to do after the gym."

"That must have been difficult." Maura pulled her jacket tighter against her body. Being a guidance counselor, she cherished the relationships she'd built with her students and took pride in seeing them succeed. She couldn't imagine working in a career where you were serving people that you never knew if you'd ever see again.

He shrugged. "It was sometimes, but I'd worked in the industry since I was a kid. It's all I knew. But that's why I wanted to buy a property like the Candle Beach Hotel. Being a part of this small-town community will be very different than working in a hotel in a huge city."

"Definitely." She stopped in front of a pretty, white house. "This is Sarah's place."

"Oh." He stared at the front window. Behind a sheer curtain, people could be seen walking around in the living room. "You weren't kidding when you said it wasn't far."

"Nope. That's one of the best things about living around here. It's not far to anything. Sarah and I can both walk to work from our houses." She gently tugged on his hand, leading him toward the door. "Ready to go in?"

"Sure."

She knocked on the door and it swung open.

"Hey." Sarah gave her a hug, then eyed Aidan. "And this must be the famous Aidan." She reached her hand out. "Hi. I'm Sarah."

He smiled and shook her hand. "Hi. Nice to meet you."

"Come in." Sarah opened the door wider. "We're still

missing Angel and Adam, but everyone else is here. My brother has a tendency to be fashionably late, but I'm sure he'll be here soon."

They entered the house. Maura stayed close to Aidan.

Patrick stepped forward. "Hi, I'm Patrick." He and Aidan shook hands.

"Nice to meet you." Aidan smiled at him and then greeted Charlotte and Luke.

"I thought we'd play charades tonight, if that's okay with everyone?" Sarah looked around, as each of them murmured their agreement.

"Sounds fun," Maura said brightly. She was usually the odd one out when they had game nights, and it was a little surreal to have Aidan standing there beside her. Earlier, she'd been reassuring Aidan, but now she was struck with a sense of uncertainty. What would her friends think of him?

"I have the game out already." Sarah gestured to the coffee table. "But would anyone like something to eat or drink before we start?" She glanced at her watch.

"I'd love something," Aidan said.

They all went into Sarah's kitchen, which was still under renovation. She'd bought the house that past December and was slowly making changes as time and funds allowed.

"I love the flooring in here." Maura admired the wide black and white patchwork of tiles.

"Thanks." Sarah smiled happily. "I thought it contrasted nicely with the apple-green walls. I'm still waiting on the new farmhouse sink, but it should be here soon. Someone ordered the wrong one the first time around." She mock-glared at Patrick, who hung his head.

"Sorry."

Sarah gently patted his shoulder and said in a teasing voice, "I forgive you, but only because you're not charging me for any of your labor in the remodel."

"That's all I am to you, huh? Cheap labor." Patrick laughed and bent down to kiss her.

Maura smiled. Usually, their public display of affection would have made her stomach twinge with unbidden jealousy, but this time she was here with someone of her own, and she could just be happy for her friend without painful feelings accompanying the emotion.

Aidan squeezed her hand and a rush of happiness came over her. He was everything she'd ever wanted in a man – thoughtful, kind, smart, and he was handsome to boot. They hadn't known each other long, but if she wasn't careful with her heart, she'd fall hopelessly in love with him – if she wasn't there already.

Her pulse quickened. Was she already in love with him? She wouldn't have expected it to happen so quickly. She didn't have much experience with love, but what they had together felt so right. She peeked up at him as he released her hand to take the glass of water Sarah was holding out to him, then looked away quickly before he caught her staring at him. Whatever this was, she didn't want it to end.

She hastily grabbed a plate and selected a few pieces from the meat, cheese and cracker tray that Sarah had set out. Then the doorbell rang, and Sarah excused herself to answer it. Maura and Aidan followed her back into the living room to see who had arrived.

Angel and Adam walked in, carrying a brown paper sack.

"Glad you could make it finally," Charlotte said to Angel as they exchanged hugs.

Angel uttered an exaggerated sigh and jutted her thumb toward Adam. "This one takes longer than any girl to get ready."

Sarah laughed. "Let me guess. He was still working on

the newspaper two seconds before you were supposed to leave?"

"Hey," Adam protested. "I had an important article to write."

Maura whispered to Aidan, "Adam owns the Candle Beach Weekly."

"Ah," he whispered back.

"We brought some cookies that I managed to hide from Adam, and a German chocolate cake that I made this morning." Angel held up the bag. "Should I put them in the kitchen?"

"I can take them in. Why don't the two of you get settled?" Sarah reached for the bag. "We're going to play charades."

"Sounds good." Adam took Angel's coat and hung both his and hers on the coat rack by the door.

Aidan stood silently behind Maura, taking it all in.

Angel flashed him a smile and held out her hand. "I'm Angel, and that's my boyfriend, Adam."

"Happy to meet you both." He shook her hand. "Aidan."

Sarah re-entered the room. "Is everyone ready to start now?"

Patrick looked around. "I think so."

"How should we divide up the teams?" Charlotte asked.

"Men against women," Luke said to her, with a gleam in his eyes. "Last time we played charades, I couldn't figure out anything you were doing."

"You're on," she retorted.

They divided into teams and using the charade words provided in the game box, they began. The women were soon several points ahead and Maura found herself laughing hilariously at Angel's depiction of an old movie. She was flapping her arms around mimicking a bird.

"The Birds!" Sarah shouted.

Angel gave a whoop. "Yep."

"Oh, man," Luke said good-naturedly. "You guys get all the easy ones."

Charlotte laughed. "We all picked randomly." She went over to him and wrapped her arm around his waist.

"Time for cake?" Sarah asked.

"Past time," Adam said, popping up from the ground. "I've been eyeing that cake for the last couple of hours." He rubbed his stomach. "It's been over two hours since I last ate."

Beside him, Angel sighed dramatically.

They all walked into the kitchen, where Sarah busied herself with making a pot of coffee while Angel cut the cake and Patrick retrieved plates from the cupboard. They were like a well-oiled machine.

"They all get along so well," Aidan said quietly to Maura. "I have to admit, I'm a little jealous."

"Me too." Maura smiled. "I haven't had friends like this since I was in grade school. Other than Sarah, I've only known the rest of them since last December, but they've welcomed me with open arms."

"Who wants a piece?" Angel held up a plate containing a huge mound of chocolate cake with coconut fudge icing.

"Me!" Adam said, reaching for it before Angel nudged him away.

Charlotte took that plate and another, and walked toward where Maura and Aidan stood near the door. "You don't want to miss out on this. Angel is famous for her cakes."

"Well, in that case, I definitely can't pass it up." Aidan smiled at her and accepted the plate. He and Maura dug into their cake.

"This is so good." He'd barely put one bite in his mouth and was already digging in for a second bite.

"Angel makes the pastries and cakes at the Bluebonnet Café." Maura couldn't help grinning at the ecstatic face he was making while eating.

"Ah. That makes sense. I've loved everything I've bought from their baked goods case." He munched on it some more. "I wonder if she'd be willing to do some baking for the hotel – or at least have the Bluebonnet Café provide us with something. I'm thinking of using one of the downstairs rooms as a small dining room."

"I'm sure she would. Angel has been talking with Maggie, our friend who owns the café, about starting her own bakery. You should ask her about it."

He licked some fudge icing off of his upper lip. "Once we get closer to opening, I definitely will."

They finished their cake and returned to playing the game, with the women thoroughly trouncing the men. Afterward, Adam and Patrick were chatting about the newspaper in the living room and Luke had pulled Aidan into a conversation with him and Charlotte, so Maura went with Angel into the kitchen.

"Do you need any help cleaning up?" Maura asked.

Sarah stood at the sink, rinsing dishes before she loaded them into the dishwasher. "I think I'm pretty good here."

"Do you want the rest of the cake?" Angel asked Sarah, nodding to the last third of the cake.

"No. It was amazing, but I'll gain twenty pounds if I eat the rest of it. Besides, I wouldn't want to deprive my brother of it."

"Not that he needs it either," Angel said. "He's been eating so much of my sweets that it's a wonder he's not diabetic by now." She sat down to put the domed lid on the plastic cake plate and securely latched the sides.

Sarah chuckled. "Our whole family has been saying that

for years, but he's as healthy as a horse." She moved over to the coffee pot. "Do you want any more coffee? I made another pot and I'll just have to throw it out if we don't drink it now."

Maura checked the clock on the wall. Ten o'clock. If she drank another cup at this time of night, she'd be up until two in the morning. Eh. It was a Saturday night and she could afford to stay up past her bedtime once in a while. Besides, she was riding so high on the fun they'd had that night and how happy she was to be with Aidan that she'd probably be up that late anyway.

"I'll take a cup."

Angel shook her head. "I'd better not. I've got an early shift at the café tomorrow."

Sarah came over to the table with mugs for herself and Maura. "I can make you some tea if you'd like?"

"Tea would be great." Angel got up from the table. "I can get my own though." She moved purposefully over to the cupboard where Sarah kept her tea and plopped a tea bag in a cup of water before heating it in the microwave.

"It'll be nice to get my hot water dispenser when the new sink comes," Sarah said as she sat down in one of the high-backed oak chairs. "It seems like a luxury, but I let Patrick talk me into it. I have to admit that I'm really looking forward to how easy it will be to make tea with instant hot water."

After Angel was seated, Sarah glanced at the door to the living room and said in a low voice to Maura, "How are things going with Aidan? I really like him."

"Me too," Maura admitted. "They're going well. It's almost like I'm waiting for the other shoe to drop though."

"Maybe there isn't another shoe." Angel sipped her tea. "Sometimes things are just meant to be. I know I had my own worries about Adam, so I don't have much room to talk, but things turned out great there. I'm sure they will for you too."

"You look happier than I've ever seen you." Sarah's eyes met Maura's. "I think he's good for you."

"I am happy. He's a great guy." She knew what she was saying was true, but it was difficult to lose control of the situation and let herself fall for him without having any fear that things could go wrong.

"Good." Sarah reached over and hugged Maura. "Don't overthink it, okay?"

Maura laughed. Her friend knew her so well. "I'll try not to."

"Ugh," Angel said. "I'd better get going. Six o'clock comes way too early in the morning."

"It is getting late. We should probably go," Maura said.

They joined the others in the living room. Aidan was still chatting with Luke and Charlotte, and Maura made her way over to him. His face was animated as he gestured with his hands. Judging by their laughter, he was telling quite a story. She didn't interrupt his tale, but enjoyed watching his expression as he spoke.

When they'd said their goodbyes and were walking along the sidewalk about a block from Sarah's house, he paused, wrapping his arm around her waist and pulling her around to face him.

"Thank you for introducing me to your friends." He sighed. "I think I needed something like this."

Her lips stretched into a wide smile as she snuggled closer to him. In the few hours that they'd been at Sarah's house, it felt as though the temperature had dropped into the low forties. "I'm glad you had fun."

"It's impossible to be unhappy when I'm around you." He touched his forehead to hers.

She closed her eyes, inhaling the intoxicating scent of

his aftershave that mingled with the crisp air. His lips touched hers, setting off a wave of sensations. It was so quiet that she could almost hear her heart beating loudly in her chest as they kissed. The night had been full of fun with friends, but being with Aidan was the best thing of all. Being near him was something she could get used to.

Sarah was right. She needed to stop overthinking everything. Chances were, things wouldn't always be perfect between her and Aidan, but she needed to live in the moment and experience what was right in front of her. She opened her eyes and looked into his. He pulled away and smiled, but held her there in front of him for a moment longer.

"It's chilly out." He rubbed his hands over her shoulders, as if to warm her. "I'd better get you home before you freeze."

She nodded, although in truth, she'd barely felt the cold.

After they'd kissed goodnight in front of her house, he waited while she unlocked her front door. She stood in the doorway, watching as he drove away. When he was gone from sight, she lightly touched her lips with her fingertip. She'd finally allowed her emotions to win out over her practical side, but he was worth it.

13

Aidan was poring over plans for the hotel when his phone rang. He reached for it, not really paying attention to what he was doing, and almost succeeded in knocking over his water bottle in the process. He caught the bottle as it teetered on the edge of the desk.

"Hello?" He tucked the phone under his chin as he flipped to the next page in his notes. Everything was more expensive than he'd planned for, but with a few changes, he should be able to make it work.

"Hey, buddy. It's Luke." Luke cleared his throat. "I'm calling to follow up on what we were talking about on game night. I talked to my sister, Zoe, and she'd love for you to come up and see the lodge she works at."

"Really?" Aidan flipped his notebook over to give Luke his full attention. "That's great. I checked it out online and it gets wonderful reviews. They must be doing something right."

Luke laughed. "According to Zoe, they're the most popular place for weddings in the Seattle area." He sobered. "Sometimes I wish they weren't because I rarely have a chance to see her."

"You could drive up with me," Aidan said. "It looks like a long drive and I wouldn't mind having someone come with me."

"I wish I could," Luke said. "But I'm working on building a covered structure for people to sit in outside of the food truck and I want to have it in place before the summer tourist traffic starts. Plus, I promised Charlotte I'd help her get the lot her trailer is on in tip-top shape too." He sighed. "I guess it's not just Zoe's fault that I don't see her very often. As soon as I'm done with the construction, I should make plans to see her."

"Did she say when she might have time for me to meet with her?" Aidan asked. He didn't know much about weddings, but he assumed spring and summer would be a popular time. "I don't want to inconvenience her."

"I'm not sure. I think she was thinking about doing it pretty soon, but you'll have to call and ask." Luke rattled off Zoe's phone number and Aidan quickly scribbled it down on an unused sheet of paper.

"Sounds good. I wish you could come up with me, but maybe Amelia will want to join me. I'll give Zoe a call. Thanks for doing this."

"No problem. I'll talk to you later."

Luke hung up. Aidan circled the phone number on his pad and then carefully dialed Zoe's number.

A bright voice came over the line. "Hello, this is Zoe Tisdale."

She sounded so perky and professional, that for a moment, Aidan wasn't sure if it was a recording or not.

"Hello?" she said again.

"Hey," he said. "This is Aidan O'Connor. I'm a friend of your brother's from Candle Beach. I recently purchased the Candle Beach Hotel, and he said you might be willing to show me around the lodge you work at so I can get some ideas for the remodel."

"Hey, Aidan." Her tone became more casual once he mentioned Luke. "Of course. I'd love to show you around. What day works for you?"

"Um. Let me check." He turned around to face the calendar he'd stuck on the wall behind the lobby's front desk. Most of the weekdays were full of appointments he'd made with sub-contractors and he needed to be at the hotel to meet them. He tapped his finger on the next empty day – Saturday. Amelia would be out of town for a design conference, but he was free. "Would Saturday work?"

"Hmm." She hesitated. "Saturdays are busy for me, but I can probably meet for an hour or so. Is that enough time?"

"I'll take whatever time you have. I just want to see the lodge and get a feel for it. Luke mentioned that the owner had worked hard to restore it to its original condition, and since I'm trying to do the same thing here at the Candle Beach Hotel, I think it would help me to see a project that's already successfully been completed." He glanced around. Things were coming together, but there was still a lot left to do on the hotel before their anticipated grand opening in June.

"I'll schedule you in for a tour at eleven, and if no major issues pop up with my work, we can probably grab lunch together afterward and chat about the lodge. Does that work for you?"

"Sounds great. I'll call to confirm the night before."

"Great. See you then." She hung up, and he scribbled the date and time on his calendar.

He'd meant what he said to Luke. Willa Bay was about four hours away, and he would have liked a travel companion to pass the time on the road. An idea came to him. Would Maura be up for it?

A thrill shot through him at the thought of spending a whole day with her. They'd been dating for a few weeks and usually spent one weekend day each week with each other, but it had always been around town. A one-day road trip could be a lot of fun.

On impulse, he picked up the phone and gave her a call.

"Hello?" She answered in a quiet voice. His heart sank. In his excitement, he'd forgotten she was at work.

"Hi. It's Aidan."

She laughed. "I know. You don't usually call me during the day. Is something wrong?"

"No. Actually, sorry about that. I didn't mean to bother you at work."

"No problem. I'm on lunch, but I'm in my office. Hold on. I'll close my office door so I don't disturb anyone else." He heard her get up and then the soft click of a door closing. "That's better," she said in a normal volume. "What's up?"

He leaned against the wall. "I was wondering if you'd like to go up to Willa Bay with me this coming Saturday."

"Willa Bay?" She paused. "Isn't that kind of far away?"

"It's about four hours each way. But I think we can easily do it in a day." He eyed his calendar. "I made plans to meet with Luke's sister to see the lodge she works at. I'm hoping to get some ideas for the hotel. Anyway, I thought it might be a fun road trip for us. We'd need to leave around seven in the morning to get there by eleven for my meeting."

"Hmm. I think I'm free, but let me check my calendar." The sound of a creaking chair and the telltale click of a computer mouse came over the line. "That should be fine." Earlier, she'd sounded hesitant, but now she was more enthusiastic.

"I'll pick you up a little before seven. We can grab breakfast on the road."

"Sounds like a plan. I haven't been on a road trip in ages."

He laughed. "Me neither. Well, I drove up here from California when I moved, but that wasn't much fun. I was trying to get here as quickly as possible and barely stopped to rest. I promise this will be more fun."

"I'll hold you to that. Bye, Aidan."

"Bye." He placed the phone on the desk.

"Why do you look so happy?" Amelia entered the lobby from outside, carrying two canvas sacks brimming with groceries. "Did we win the lottery?"

He eyed his notebook. The construction totals were just as high as they had been when he'd last seen them. "I wish. No, I just made plans with Maura to take a trip up to Willa Bay to meet with Luke's sister and check out the hotel there."

"Hey, what about me? I would have gone. I hear the tulips up there are gorgeous this time of year." She pouted at him.

"Zoe wanted to meet on Saturday and you'll be gone."

"Oh, fine, toss logic at me." She smiled at him. "So, you'll be spending the day with Maura."

"Uh-huh." His face warmed.

"You've been spending a lot of time with her." She peered at him. "You must really like her."

He sighed. "I do. I didn't expect to meet anyone like her in Candle Beach, especially so soon after we got here, but I'm glad I did."

"You look happy," she observed. "Since Mom and Dad died, you've been in a funk, but this is good for you."

"Thanks for that analysis." He smirked. "Maybe you'll find your match up here too."

She snorted loudly. "I doubt it."

"You never know." Meeting Maura hadn't been on his agenda, but fate had other plans for them.

"Oh, I do know. I'm way too picky. I'll probably die an old maid." She gestured to the kitchen. "I'd better get the groceries put away."

"Do you need any help?"

"I think I can manage," she said dryly. "I grabbed some sandwich fixings for lunch if you want anything. You've been working on your plans all morning. You should eat something."

"Thanks, Amelia." He shook his head as she left the room. Amelia had inherited their mother's love for taking care of people – something that often annoyed him when she was so sure she knew what was best for him. This time, however, it was appreciated. He had been working hard. This day trip would be a good opportunity for him to get out and relax a little, even if it was for work reasons.

14

"Do you want me to turn on the air-conditioning?" Aidan asked, turning his head slightly toward where Maura sat in the passenger seat.

"Nope, this is great. You picked a perfect day for a trip to Willa Bay." She relaxed against the back of the seat, taking in the scenery as it flashed by. She'd lived in Washington for a while now, but rarely ventured away from the coast. When she did, it was usually to drive to the airport to head home to San Francisco for the holidays. Now, without the responsibility of driving, she was able to see the long stretches of rural areas, trees, and the mudflats formed by the receding tide.

He chuckled. "I didn't have much of a choice. Zoe has a tight schedule with all of the weddings she manages on the weekends."

"Are you sure she's okay with me coming too?" Maura shifted her body to look at him better. She'd never met Zoe before, and she wasn't sure it was appropriate for her to tag along to Aidan's business meeting. She forced her breathing to slow. If it didn't work out for her to meet with Zoe too, she could always hang out somewhere else in town.

He smiled. "I called her yesterday to confirm our appointment and asked if it was okay if I brought you. She said she was happy to meet you too, especially because you're friends with Charlotte." He flipped on the CD player. "Is Fleetwood Mac okay?"

"Yep. My mom loves them, so I grew up listening to their songs." Maura leaned back in her seat again. She hadn't known what to expect, being stuck in a car with Aidan for several hours, but it was going well.

They chatted for a few hours about music, their parents, and growing up in the Bay Area. They were making good time until they hit Seattle and she worried they'd be late for their appointment with Zoe. Soon though, the heavy traffic cleared and they were coasting along on the freeway again, heading north. When the exit for Willa Bay appeared, the scenery had turned to farmlands, and she spotted a lone farmhouse and acreage next to the road. It must have been difficult for the owners to have had their land bisected when the interstate was built. She shut her eyes for a moment as Aidan took the exit and the road curved, imagining what things must have been like before the freeway came through.

When she opened them, she didn't have to imagine what it would have looked like. They were on a small country road, with fields as far as she could see. The farms were interspersed with barns and houses, and there were more cows and horses than people. Around the next turn, the green fields gave way to a riot of color.

She gasped and rolled down her window to look closer. "Are those tulips?"

He grinned and eyed the clock on the dashboard. "Yup. Zoe told me Willa Bay is famous not only for their weddings, but for their tulips as well." His attention turned back to the road as he navigated a sharp curve. "I thought we'd take a tour of one of the fields after our meeting, if that's alright with you."

She couldn't take her eyes off the flowers. "I love tulips. I had no idea there were fields here in Washington. I always think of them as being from Holland."

"Me too." He checked the directions he'd scribbled on a Post-it note and made a left at the next intersection. "It makes me wish I had time to explore more of the state."

"I'm sure there will be time once the renovation is complete."

The tulip fields disappeared and were replaced with a more populated area and the scent of saltwater.

"Are we near Puget Sound?" she asked, straining to see past the next bend in the road.

"I'd have to look at a map to be sure, but I believe Willa Bay is on Puget Sound." He took another left, and she started to catch glimpses of blue water through the trees. Soon they pulled up in front of a large wooden structure, with an artfully composed sign reading *Willa Bay Lodge*.

Maura felt as though she'd been transported to another world. Elegant stone-lined pathways forked off from the main walkways and disappeared into lush gardens.

"Wow. This place is gorgeous."

He nodded, maneuvering around a vehicle that had stopped in the circular driveway with its motor running, and then pulled into an empty parking space. He quickly exited the car and came around to her side to open the door.

"Thanks." She stepped out into a warm April breeze. The scent of gardenias floated in the air and she inhaled deeply while stretching her legs a bit. "Ah. It feels good to move around."

He smiled and checked his watch. "We've got about fifteen minutes before we're supposed to meet with Zoe. Do you want to check the place out first?"

She nodded. "I'd love to see where those paths lead. I feel like I'm in a secret garden or something. You should definitely put some gardens in at the hotel."

"I don't know. Maybe a few rosebushes or something. I don't want to go too crazy," he said dubiously.

"Trust me," she said. "They'll add a ton of color, and the guests will love them."

He shrugged. "I'll think about it."

They set out on one of the stone pathways, following it along as it wound around the side of the lodge, coming out behind the back deck.

"And I thought the front of the lodge was nice." Maura felt her eyes widen as she gazed at the wide expanse of water in front of them. She turned to get a better view of the back deck. "This is similar to the one at the Candle Beach Hotel."

"I think so too." He narrowed his eyes, as if taking in the details. "Those picture windows are fantastic, although I don't really want to mess with the structure of the Great Room's windows. I like the curtains they've got up on the far end though. I bet they keep some of the breeze off the water away from the guests."

Several guests were sitting on the deck in white Adirondack chairs, similar to the ones at the Candle Beach Hotel. Some of them were relaxing with the news-paper, while others were enjoying a beverage and snack outside.

"We'd better find the lobby. I told Zoe we'd meet her at the front desk." Aidan scanned the building and pointed to a door at the end of the seating area. "I think we can go in through there."

She followed him inside. They walked through a room with tall ceilings, a large fireplace and cushion-topped log sofas. The overall affect was of simple grandeur and relaxation. Spending a few nights in this hotel was definitely going on her bucket list.

When they'd reached the front desk, Aidan gave the attendant his name, and she disappeared into a back room, returning with a dark-haired woman in her thirties.

"Hi, I'm Zoe, and you must be Aidan and Maura. It's so nice to meet you both." She held out her hand to them and smiled warmly. "Luke has told me a lot about you. I wish I could get back home and meet the rest of the gang that he talks about so much."

"I know he'd love that," Aidan said as he shook her hand. "He told me he wished he could have come up here this weekend, but he's working on a big project at home and couldn't get away."

Zoe sighed. "He's always busy. But I'm glad he's so happy there in Candle Beach. He never seemed too happy when he was in California."

"The pace of life is much slower in Candle Beach," Aidan agreed. "I recently moved up here from California too, and although it's very different, I'm finding I enjoy it." He smiled at Maura. "And the people in town aren't half bad either."

She mock-glared at him. "You're growing on us too."

Zoe shook her head. "Sometimes I really miss Haven Shores." She motioned in the direction of the water. "Being by the water here is similar, but not quite the same as the open ocean. I love my job and have no intention of moving back anytime soon, but I do miss Luke and Pops." She sighed. "Anyway, you wanted a tour of the lodge, right? Is there anything in particular you'd like to see?"

"I was hoping to see some of the guest rooms and maybe some of the common areas. We've already toured part of the gardens. They're quite impressive."

She laughed. "I'll let our landscaping crew know that you said that. Alright then. Let's start out upstairs, and then we can come back down here where I can show you the main guest areas."

She walked quickly toward a staircase that was almost hidden off of the main lobby area. "We don't have an elevator, and while there are some guest rooms on the main floor that we reserve for those who need more accessible accommodations, the bulk of the guest rooms are on the second floor."

They climbed up the stairs, which were covered by a low-pile red rug with a blue floral print. The stairs were wide and had a large landing halfway up.

"Your staff must get a good workout, climbing these stairs all the time," Aidan said. "I considered installing an elevator at the hotel, but the cost was prohibitive."

She nodded. "I believe they considered an elevator here, but opted not to put one in due to cost. Plus, I think it kind of adds to the charm of the lodge. It's just like it was when it was first built." She approached a room and flashed a key card against a black box on the wall. "We've made some upgrades though for safety reasons."

She pushed the door open to reveal a sizable light-filled room. A king-sized bed with a lavender bedspread was situated against one wall. A painting of a dark purple tulip hung over it.

"This is a standard room, although each room is a little different, with different color combinations. We've gone with a tulip theme, as we're in tulip country and the guests seem to love it."

The bed was piled high with plump pillows and Maura had a sudden urge to flop out on it. They'd left early and it had been a long drive. A nap was sounding pretty good at the moment and she couldn't imagine a nicer place to take one. To quell the sleepiness, she walked over to the window and peered out. They were so close to Puget Sound that she could see birds diving into the water to retrieve fishes. "Do all of the rooms have a view?"

Zoe straightened a bouquet of fresh tulips on the dresser. "They all have a view, whether of the bay itself, or of the gardens. Although some of our guests always request the water view, I'm partial to the gardens myself. Maybe because I spend so much time in them, working with my bridal clients on their ideal ceremonies."

"Everything here is beautiful. I can't imagine a more beautiful location for a wedding," Maura said.

"Good." Zoe grinned. "That's what we're going for. If people didn't feel that way, I wouldn't have a job as a wedding coordinator."

She led them out of the room and showed them a few more of the unoccupied rooms. As she'd said, they were all fairly similar in layout, and although they'd chosen different bedframes and decorating schemes, all of the rooms included tulips in the motifs. The bathrooms were just as nice as the rest of the room, with luxury showers with rain-fall showerheads and jetted bathtubs. This place probably cost more for a night than she made in a week at the middle school.

"Is there anything else you'd like to see up here?" Zoe asked as she closed the door of the last room they'd seen. "We have a small library on this floor, but most of the common rooms are on the main floor."

"I'd like to see the library," Aidan said. "The library at my hotel is currently in the Great Room, but I'm thinking of moving it to a different location and combining it with a business center."

"Sure. It's right this way."

The library had French doors with small glass panes and was larger than it looked from the outside, although it still had a cozy feel.

"Was this originally a guest room?" Maura asked. It was around the size of the other rooms they'd seen.

Zoe shook her head. "I don't think so. It may have served another purpose before, but I've seen some photos of the library in use in the 1920s and it's always been in this location. They may have just wanted a quiet space upstairs for people to relax in if it was too noisy in the other common areas."

She took them downstairs and briefly showed them the kitchen, the rest of the large hall, and the smaller dining area. "This is one of the most popular features of the lodge – it's where we serve our famous breakfast every morning. Our chef is well known for his innovative dinners as well."

Aidan circled the room, making notes on his phone. "Have you found that this is a good size for a dining area, or does it seem small sometimes?"

The room only held about ten tables for two or four, but the lodge itself wasn't large. A few couples were happily eating lunch in front of one of the two floor-to-ceiling windows overlooking the bay.

Zoe waved at one of the couples, who waved back at her. "Once in a while, we have a larger event and we host it in the main hall, but usually, this is fine. We don't have that many rooms and people can make reservations for dining times, so it's normally not a problem. Of course, for wedding receptions, we usually use a large banquet tent on the lawn."

"Hmm." He made some more notes. "I was considering creating something similar at the hotel, but I wasn't sure about the size. I think the space I have should work though. I'm so glad to have had this opportunity to meet with you."

"Of course." She smiled and gestured to the tables. "I

don't have anything else for you to see, but can I interest you in some lunch? It's on the house."

Maura's mouth watered. She'd been eying the steak and blue cheese salad one of the women was eating. The snacks they'd eaten in the car seemed a long-ago memory.

Aidan seemed to catch her expression, and he winked at her. "We'd love to have lunch here."

Zoe smiled. "Great. I'll go find us a table for three." She left them in the entrance to the dining area and walked over to talk to the hostess.

After lunch, they said goodbye to Zoe, extracting a promise from her to come visit Candle Beach soon, then retreated to Aidan's car.

Maura twisted in her seat. "Do you think you can recreate that ambience at the hotel?"

"I hope so." He frowned. "I thought I was prepared for this, but seeing the Willa Bay Lodge, I'm realizing there are so many things that I need to consider."

"Are you worried about it?" Maura asked. Aidan didn't usually express concern about the hotel renovations or about running it in the future.

An uneasy smile came over his face. "Maybe a little. Sometimes I worry that Amelia and I have bitten off more than we can chew."

"Is there anything I can do? I know people around town would be happy to help too."

"No. I'm sure we'll be fine." His characteristic easygoing smile replaced his doubtful expression. "The magnitude of the project just hits me once in a while."

"But once the hotel is finished, all you'll have to do is operate it, right? There's an end in sight."

"I guess." He turned to gaze back at the lodge. "But there are so many people involved in the operation here. Now that

I've made improvements in the hotel, investors have started popping up out of the woodwork to make offers on the property."

Maura looked up at him sharply. "You're not thinking of taking one of their offers though, right?"

His eyes flickered for a moment. "No. Not right now. Amelia and I took on this project with the expectation that we'd manage it in the future. For now, that's still the plan."

"Oh." Maura leaned back in her seat, silent.

Aidan started the car and slowly drove out of the parking lot. The lodge had seemed magical when they'd first arrived, but after Aidan's admittance of uncertainty, it had taken on a feeling of unease.

Before heading home, they drove to a tulip field, bought some bulbs, and took some pictures, but her heart wasn't in it.

"Are you okay?" Aidan asked when they were back in the car.

"I'm fine. Just a little tired," she lied. She turned her head to the side and stared out the window as the tulip fields disappeared from view, replaced by the concrete expanse of the interstate.

Aidan took his eyes off the road for a second to look at Maura, asleep in the passenger seat next to him. He wasn't sure why, but the jovial atmosphere they'd had earlier on their road trip had disappeared. After they left the lodge, she'd become quiet, not even perking up when they were in the tulip fields. He'd thought for sure that she'd love seeing all of the tulips and had been excited about sharing them with her.

She shifted in her seat, but her eyes didn't open. Traffic was light, and they made it through Seattle quickly. He'd been in Candle Beach for only a few months and already had forgotten how much he hated city traffic. It would be good to be back home soon. Home. How quickly he'd come to think of Candle Beach as home.

He was fairly certain that he and Amelia had made the right decision to purchase the hotel, but his trip to Willa Bay had given him a great deal to think about. When he'd worked as a manager at a large hotel in the city, he hadn't been in charge of everything involving the hotel. Although he and Amelia worked together on the hotel, most of the daily operations fell on him and he was feeling the strain of the responsibility.

He'd received several offers from investors and had turned them all down immediately. Now, a small part of him wondered if those decisions had been made too hastily. Was this what he wanted for the rest of his life? A hotel in a small town on the Washington coast?

The sun seared into his eyes and he pulled down the visor, momentarily distracted from his thoughts. It was enough to make him realize that this wasn't a decision to be made anytime soon. He'd made a commitment to see the renovations of the hotel through and he'd honor that commitment. After that, he'd see.

Maura stretched in her sleep, and his heart melted. He hadn't expected to meet her or to fall in love. Love. Was he really in love with her? They hadn't been together for long, but there was something about her that had captivated him the moment he met her. Her eyes had been full of passion as she decried his purchase of the hotel and a little part of him had fallen for her right then.

What would he do if he sold the hotel? If he didn't own it, there was no reason to stay in Candle Beach. Long-distance relationships were difficult, and he didn't know if he and Maura would be ready for one. He cast a glance at her again. He'd tried to hide his uncertainty over the future of the hotel, but had she noticed it? Was she worried about their future as well? Was that why her mood had soured so fast?

She stirred again and her eyes fluttered open.

"Good afternoon, Sleeping Beauty." A grin slid over his lips. Her hair was mussed and her face flushed, but she was still beautiful.

She sat up straight and ran her fingers through her thick, dark hair. "How long was I out?"

"Oh, you were sawing logs for about forty-five minutes."

"I was?" She stiffened. "Why didn't you wake me up? I'm so embarrassed."

He laughed. "I'm joking. I think you were out for close to an hour, but you weren't snoring. We'll be home in about an hour and a half."

She nodded. "Good. Uh, do you think we could take a stretch break soon? I must have been sleeping funny because my legs are starting to hurt."

"I think there's a rest stop up ahead."

They pulled off at the rest stop, and after using the facilities, they walked down to the small creek behind the building. A breeze rustled the tree branches above them and birds chirped. Water bubbled lazily through rocks in the creek, creating a Zen-like experience.

"It's almost like we're out hiking," Maura said. "I can't believe we're so close to the freeway."

As if in response, a semi-truck roared past. They both laughed and he was happy to see she was feeling better. Before they set off on the final leg of the journey, he grabbed some sodas out of the ice chest and gave one to her.

"Ah. This is nice and cold." Maura gulped her root beer.

"Do you need a snack or anything?" He stuck his hand into the snack bag and rustled it around in there. "I think we've got some chips, crackers, and beef jerky left."

"I'm good, thanks." She set the soda pop can in her cup holder. "I will be happy to get home though. This has been a long day."

"Are you doing okay?" His eyes searched her face.

She gave him a funny look. "Yeah. Why?"

"Oh, nothing."

She stared at him.

"You got quiet after we left the lodge and have barely spoken a word to me since, even when we were in the tulip fields."

She looked away, then met his gaze. "I'm just tired. Sorry if I wasn't in better spirits. I did love the tulip field."

He smiled. "I'm glad you enjoyed it. I was probably imagining something where it wasn't."

She gave him a wan smile and turned to fasten her seatbelt.

Although she wasn't as chatty as usual, they did talk some on the rest of the way home, mainly about her family and her job as a school counselor. Still though, she wasn't acting like her normal cheery self. Something he'd said or done had changed her attitude and he wasn't sure what it had been. He hoped it wasn't from telling her that he was worried about the hotel.

If it was because of that, he'd have to make sure not to repeat that mistake again. He didn't want to do anything that could jeopardize their relationship. If keeping quiet about the things that were bothering him was what it took, that's what he'd need to do.

When they arrived back at her home, she jumped out of the car and headed inside before he had a chance to walk her to her door. Something was definitely wrong. He drove back to the hotel and parked, but instead of going back to work, he went down the stairs to the beach and set out across the sand. Maybe after the long car ride, the physical exercise would help to clear his brain and figure out how to make things right with Maura.

15

Maura stewed on her concerns about Aidan for the first part of the week, somehow managing to avoid talking to him. By Thursday, she was so frustrated with herself for spinning in circles that she knew she needed to talk to a friend. The bookstore was a good place to start because she could usually catch Dahlia or Sarah at work there.

However, when she arrived at the bookstore, her heart sank. Sarah was working, but she had a line at the register, and the place was packed. Sarah saw her enter and waved at her before turning back to the customer she was helping. Dahlia wasn't in the sales area, so Maura went to the back to see if she was in her office.

Her office door was open and the light was off. Maura almost left, but she noticed the door to Charlotte's apartment above the bookstore was open. She climbed the stairs and knocked on the door at the top.

"Charlotte? Are you home?"

"Hold on," Charlotte called out. She appeared at the door a moment later, holding a barbecued chicken leg in her hand. "Hey, Maura."

"Sorry to bother you, but I wanted to bounce something off a friend." Maura glanced up as a shadow moved behind Charlotte. "Is someone else here?"

"Just Luke. Come in."

"Oh, no, it looks like you're having dinner. I don't want to interrupt your date."

Charlotte laughed. "No worries. He brought over some leftovers from work for dinner. We were talking about going to Haven Shores to see a movie, but nothing that's playing looks good to me."

"Are you sure?" Maura peered past her.

"Come in," Luke said, appearing behind Charlotte. "We have a ton of food. Are you hungry?"

The sweet and spicy scent of barbecue wafted out of the apartment.

"It does smell good," Maura admitted. "Are you sure you don't mind?"

"We're sure." Charlotte grabbed Maura's arm with her free hand and pulled her up the last stair.

Maura fixed herself a plate of barbecue, corn on the cob, mashed potatoes, and cornbread muffins. Although this wasn't the girl talk she'd hoped for, if nothing else, the food would be comforting and delicious. Luke pulled the small square table away from the wall to make more room, and Charlotte fetched a chair from her bedroom.

"I think this is the most guests I've ever had in here." Charlotte smiled as she sat down, then took a bite of corn-bread muffin.

"Well, thank you for inviting me in. This looks amazing." Maura dug into her food. She wasn't sure if she wanted to get into her dilemma about Aidan with Luke present.

When they were almost finished, Charlotte eyed her. "What's up with you? Is something wrong?"

Maura put down the corn she'd been eating and wiped

her mouth with a paper napkin. "It's no big deal. Don't worry about it."

Luke and Charlotte exchanged glances, and he stood from the table. "I should get going. I'll leave you and Charlotte to your girl talk."

Maura's gut wrenched. Now she was ruining their date. "No. I should go." She stood to leave, then sat back down. Luke had known Aidan longer than she had. Maybe he'd have some good advice for her. "You know, actually, maybe it would help for me to talk with both of you."

Luke sat back down. "What's going on?"

"It's Aidan." She looked down at her almost empty plate. "Things were going well with him and then something happened that really bothered me."

Charlotte raised an eyebrow. "What happened?"

"Well, you know how he's been renovating the hotel, right? It turns out he's received offers on it from investors. When we were up in Willa Bay, he mentioned them."

"Is he going to sell the hotel?" Charlotte closed up a food container in front of her.

"He said no," Maura said slowly. "But I don't know. He mentioned being homesick too and how the hotel has cost more in time and energy than he expected."

Charlotte and Luke looked at each other.

"And the idea of him selling upsets you?" Luke asked.

"Yeah." She fiddled with her barbecue sauce stained napkin. "The hotel is important to me – and to Candle Beach's history. If someone else buys it, I don't know that they'll honor that history, the way Aidan promised to do."

"And what about Aidan leaving?" Charlotte prodded.

Maura felt herself crumble and she slumped down in her chair. "I don't want him to leave," she whispered.

"I don't think he wants to leave you any more than you want him to go," Luke said. "I haven't talked to him in a while, but honestly, the move to Candle Beach and having you in his life have been so good for him."

"Then why would he want to leave?" Maura asked in a small voice. She'd thought she was upset with Aidan because of a potential change in ownership of the hotel, but was she more concerned about him leaving her? "Things were so good between us."

"Oh, sweetie." Charlotte hugged her. "I don't think he's doing this because he doesn't have feelings for you. Maybe he's just overwhelmed with everything. This is a huge project he's undertaken."

"You know, back when he and I were both working in the Bay Area, Aidan never had much time for women. He was always so driven with his career. Three years ago, I could see him selling a hotel he'd bought if he could get more money for it. After his parents died though, things changed for him. I think he slowed down a little and really evaluated what he wanted out of life. His definition of success has changed." Luke cleared the food off the table and placed the containers in the refrigerator.

"I thought what he wanted was the Candle Beach Hotel." Had Aidan's dreams changed?

"If that's true," Charlotte said, "thinking about selling must be extremely difficult for him. I doubt he's taking any decision about this lightly."

"You should talk to him," Luke said simply. "I think things might look different if you let him know how you feel."

Maura looked at them. They were right. She'd been torturing herself, wondering how she felt about everything, but only talking to Aidan would help. She pushed herself up from the table.

"Thanks, you guys – for the food and for the advice."

She laughed. "Usually I'm the one giving the guidance, so this is a whole new realm for me."

Charlotte smiled. "No problem. We both want the best for you."

Luke nodded in agreement, but stayed silent.

Charlotte stood and moved over to Maura, giving her another hug. "Let me know if there's anything else I can do, okay?"

"Thanks." Maura said her goodbyes to them and walked slowly down the stairs to the bookstore. Sarah was still slammed with customers, so Maura waved goodbye to her and left. She wanted to believe what Charlotte and Luke had said – that she and the hotel were important to Aidan – but she didn't know if she was ready to talk to him and find out for sure.

Before their trip to Willa Bay, they'd made plans to go out on a date on Friday night. At this point, she wasn't sure that was something she could do. She had another day to decide though, and maybe things would look brighter in the morning.

Friday night came all too quickly, and instead of being out on a fun date with Aidan, Maura found herself leaning back against the soft pillows of her living room couch, hugging her knees to her chest. Barker climbed up on the couch next to her, softly nudging at her hand with his cold nose. She reached out to pet him, which he took as an invitation to settle himself closer to her.

She'd made some excuse to Aidan about why she couldn't make their date that evening. She'd sent him a text, and he hadn't responded – not that she'd thought he would. It had been a pretty lame excuse, but she still wasn't sure how she felt about him or what she wanted to do about their relationship. His admission that he was considering selling the hotel had seemingly come out of nowhere, and it had hurt.

Talking with Charlotte had seemed like a good plan, but now she was more conflicted than ever. Maybe Charlotte and Luke had been right – she needed to talk to Aidan about it.

She eased Barker off her lap and stood from the couch, shaking out her partially numb legs. He peered up at her.

"Sorry, buddy. I have to go talk to someone."

He dropped his head to the couch and curled up for a nap. She watched him for a moment. If only life was as easy for humans as it was for dogs.

During the few minutes it took for her to get to the hotel, she changed her mind three times about talking to Aidan. When she was about to pull into the driveway of the hotel, she finally straightened her shoulders and decided she couldn't put it off any longer. She wasn't sure what to expect from Aidan when she talked to him, but if she waited, she ran the chance of having her heart broken.

16

"Hey," Amelia said, coming around to the front of the high-backed chair Aidan was sitting in near the Great Room's tall windows. "What are you doing here? I thought you had a date with Maura." She carried with her two mugs of coffee.

"I thought I did too, but she canceled." He picked up an envelope that had already been opened, sliding the contents out onto the table in front of him to join the other bills he'd been reviewing.

"Oh, no. Is she not feeling well?" Amelia sat down across from him, setting a cup of coffee next to the stack of bills. He felt her eyes on his face. He didn't really want to get into the reasons Maura hadn't shown up for their date, but he knew Amelia wouldn't let go easily.

"As far as I know, she's feeling fine. She gave me some flimsy excuse about needing to work on a craft project at home. She didn't even call me, just sent me a text to let me know she wasn't coming over tonight." He stared out the window. The sun was low in the sky and would soon set. Usually, the scenery cheered him, but today it did nothing to raise his spirits.

Amelia raised an eyebrow. "Maybe she really did have to get it done. I can't see Maura blowing you off for something that wasn't important."

Aidan leaned forward, catching his head in his hands. He wearily rubbed his eyes, then looked up at his sister. "I think she wants to break up with me."

"What do you mean? I thought everything was going well between the two of you." She scooted her chair closer to him.

"I did too – until we went on that trip to Willa Bay." He sighed. "Something happened that day, and other than the text she sent to cancel our date, she hasn't talked to me since. I don't know what it was."

"What did you do?"

"Nothing!" He sighed. "I mean, I don't think I did anything wrong, but maybe she took something I said the wrong way. I may have mentioned that we'd received some offers on the hotel. It seemed like it was after that point that her attitude toward me changed." The strong aroma of freshly brewed coffee wafted through the air and he took a sip of it. The acid on his tongue made his stomach churn, and he immediately put the cup down. With everything else going on, he didn't know how to handle Maura being upset with him.

"Oh. I can see how that could be upsetting to her." She sat back thoughtfully. "Did you talk with her about it?"

"No. She just shut down on the ride home and barely talked to me." He fidgeted with the pen in his hands. "I had this perfect day planned and had surprised her with a trip to the tulip fields. I was going to tell her I loved her."

"Whoa." She sat upright. "You're that serious about her?"

He nodded, overcome with emotion. Had he lost Maura before he'd even had a chance to tell her how he felt?

"You need to figure out what's wrong between the two of you."

"I know." His attention drifted back to the hotel's finances. "But right now, I don't know what to tell her. Maybe we should accept one of the offers we've received."

Her eyes drilled into him. "Do you want to sell the hotel? I thought this was what you wanted. I mean, we'd talked about it for so long."

"It was." He glanced at the bills on the table and she followed his gaze. "I mean, it is. I don't know. It's all such a mess now. Everything here is costing twice as much as we'd budgeted." He picked up a letter on the top of the pile and held it out to his sister. "Remember how the electrician told us we'd need to update the wiring? Well, he's recommending a complete re-wire of the entire hotel."

She took the document from him and scanned it. He knew when she'd reached the total, because her jaw dropped. "How can it possibly be this expensive?"

"It just is." He held up the thick stack of bills, the pages feathering out in the air. "None of these are good news for us. Maybe selling the hotel would be for the best."

"Why didn't you say anything before?" Amelia asked.

He ran his fingers through his hair. "At first, things were going to plan, with only a few items coming in over budget. Then it snowballed. I was going to tell you this weekend, once I had the final estimate for the electric work."

He checked her expression, hoping she wasn't angry with him. Her face was poker straight as she looked at the paper again and then back at him.

"Okay," she said slowly. "Do we have enough money to finish the project?"

"At this point, I don't know." He gestured to the notebook where he wrote down all of the bills. Using a computer would have been easier, but he liked the tactile feeling of using pen and paper – it helped him think. "We can afford the bills we have currently, but if anything else goes over, we could be in trouble." Blood pounded in his ears. They couldn't afford any other issues with the hotel.

"Ouch. I don't like the sound of that." She took a deep breath. "What are we going to do about it?"

"I don't know." He'd been thinking through a few options, but none of them seemed good. Perhaps it had been for the best that Maura hadn't come over. His head wasn't in the right place right now and he wouldn't be very good company.

"If we sell, would we be able to recoup our investment?" Amelia asked.

"Yes. Even with all of the expenses, a sale would be profitable. Now that we've got the place in fairly good shape, investors have taken notice and decided that it would be a good investment after all."

"Do you want to sell?" she asked, adding quickly, "I'm okay with whatever you decide. I know this was our dream, but it's not worth it if it's turned into our nightmare."

"Thanks." He smiled faintly at her, his eyes tearing over. It was good to know that his sister was in his corner and would support him, no matter what he decided about selling the hotel. If only he could get Maura on his side as well. He needed to make her understand how much he loved her.

The faint noise of footsteps on tile came from the lobby, and the two of them exchanged glances.

"Were you expecting someone?" he asked Amelia.

"Nope. You?"

He shook his head and strode out of the room with her close on his heels. With any luck, it wouldn't be a bill collector.

"Hi." Maura couldn't quite make herself look Aidan in the eyes when he entered the lobby.

"Hi." He paused several feet away from her. Stillness hung in the air as they silently regarded each other.

"Uh, hi, Maura." Amelia edged past Aidan, moving toward the door to the owner's part of the hotel. She pointed at it. "Um, I've got some stuff to take care of in there, but we're still on for tomorrow, right?" She scurried into the kitchen before Maura could respond to her greeting and confirm the meeting they'd planned for Saturday.

When they were alone, Aidan spoke first.

"I thought you had a craft project you were working on at home – that was why you couldn't make our date." He leaned against the front desk.

She met his gaze. "No. I'm sorry. I wasn't telling you the truth."

He moved closer. "Okay, then what is the truth? Did you just not want to go out with me tonight?"

She took a deep breath. "You may have noticed I've been avoiding you."

He nodded, but let her speak.

"I'm worried that you don't seem as devoted to the hotel project as you were before, or to the idea of staying in Candle Beach. You made a few comments when we went to Willa Bay about how nice it was up there and how you might want to live there someday."

"I did say that in passing. But that doesn't mean I'm not devoted to the Candle Beach Hotel." He folded his arms across his chest.

"True, but what you did say was that you've had offers on the hotel. You didn't tell me outright that you weren't going to accept them, so I know you're thinking about it. That tells me that you have doubts about staying here in Candle Beach." In a smaller voice, she said, "Or doubts about our relationship." She eyed him. "I need to know where you stand. Do you want to sell the hotel or not?"

"What does any of this have to do with our relationship?" he asked. "I thought things were going well between us."

"You told me that you were committed to the hotel. You know how much it means to me that it doesn't fall into the hands of some developer. I feel like you were misleading me if you were considering selling it all along."

He shot her an incredulous look. "Misleading you?" He pressed his hands together in front of his chin. "Of course I'm considering selling the hotel. I have no other choice." His face reddened as he swept his hands around to angrily gesture at everything in the room. "I'm drowning here and you aren't making it any better."

"Drowning?" she said in a low voice. "Is that what you think of our relationship?"

Her heart felt as though it were breaking into a million tiny pieces and she fought to keep the tears at bay. Something was obviously going on with Aidan, and he hadn't shared it with her.

"Right now, yeah. Not everything is about you." He spun in a half circle, then turned back to face her, his expression contrite. "I'm sorry, I didn't mean that."

By this time, she couldn't hold back the tears. "I think you did."

She rushed out of the room as sobs wracked her body. She got into her car and drove home on autopilot, parking alongside the curb outside her house. It had started to rain, and she stared blindly through the rain-streaked windshield. Aidan wasn't who she'd thought he was. Grabbing a Kleenex from the box on the passenger seat, she dabbed at her eyes and was hit with a sudden realization.

He was exactly as she'd originally assumed – ready to make a quick buck when the situation presented itself. Thank goodness she'd found that out before it was too late. With that thought, waves of emotional pain slammed into her with the weight of a Mack truck.

She was wrong about that too. It already was too late – she'd fallen in love with someone who obviously didn't feel the same for her. She sat in the car, crying until she had no tears left, then ran through the rain to her house. At least Barker would be happy to see her.

Aidan watched Maura leave, his stomach twisting more the farther away she got. What had just happened? Everything had seemingly been going well with their relationship, and then it was like a light switch had been flipped.

Unfortunately, he knew the answer to his question. It was his fault. He'd allowed his concerns and stress about the hotel's finances to get the better of him and he'd snapped at her. As soon as he'd seen her standing there, his first thought had been to tell her how much he loved her and didn't want to lose her. He'd lost track of what he'd wanted to say when she accused him of purposefully misleading her. It had never been his intention to mislead her, and her accusation had cut him deeply.

Still though, that was no reason for him to have reacted the way he did. He should have stayed calm and tried to reason with her – tried to make her understand what was going on in his life.

A clap of thunder jarred him away from his thoughts, and the sky opened up. Rain poured to the ground, splashing against the front porch. Reluctantly, he turned away from where he'd last seen Maura and walked inside.

The most recent offer for the hotel, which Parker had presented to him that morning, lay on the front desk, right where Aidan had left it. He'd only looked at it once, and the sheaf of paper was flat and pristine. He picked it up, read the offer quickly, then set it back down on the desk. He paced the lobby, then walked into the Great Room and flopped into the chair he'd been sitting in facing the mounds of debts they owed. He leaned back and stared at the ceiling.

If he and Amelia accepted the offer, they'd realize a tidy profit on the hotel and it would make all of their money worries disappear. But was it worth it? The Candle Beach Hotel was exactly what they'd talked about buying for years. Yes, managing the renovations was much more difficult and spendy than they'd initially thought. But if they were lucky and careful with their funds, they could make it work, especially if they could get the hotel open by the summer to take advantage of the tourist traffic.

He looked up, allowing his attention to turn to the sheet of rain that almost obscured the view of the Pacific Ocean, but couldn't conceal the waves pounding on the sand. Even in poor weather, it was beautiful. This was why people flocked to the ocean in the winter to watch the powerful winter storms. He'd fallen in love with the hotel and with the Washington Coast the first time he visited Candle Beach. There had to be a reason that life had brought him there.

17

The morning after their break-up, Maura had never felt more reluctant to drive to the Candle Beach Hotel. Seeing Aidan was the last thing she wanted to do, but she'd made plans with Amelia to go over some final details for the renovations. She crossed her fingers as she held onto the steering wheel. Maybe he wouldn't even be there.

When she arrived at the hotel, she breathed a sigh of relief. Only Amelia's blue Toyota was in the parking lot. She grabbed her bag containing the photo albums that Aidan had returned to her a few weeks prior, and got out of the car, drinking in the warm breeze coming off of the ocean. It ruffled her hair and she swept a hand across her head to tame the errant strands. Although it had stormed the night before, just like that, the weather had changed, bringing them a sunny morning. Summer would be here before she knew it. It had been a long winter and spring, and she was looking forward to warmer weather and time off from her work at the schools.

The lobby door was ajar when she reached it, so she pushed it in without knocking. Amelia sat at the front desk, staring at something on her laptop computer.

She flashed Maura a warm smile. "Hey. I'm glad you could make it. You didn't look so good last night. Are you doing better today?"

A heat rose in Maura's cheeks. Facing Amelia was worse than she'd anticipated. Had Aidan told his sister about their break-up?

"I'm feeling a little better." Her stomach twisted at her words. She may not have been physically sick last night, but ending her relationship with Aidan had been one of the most difficult things she'd ever had to do. She'd thought they had a future together, and it hurt to think that now they never would.

Amelia gestured for Maura to follow her into the Great Room, where she led her over to the grouping of chairs near the window. Maura sat, hugging her bag to her chest.

"Aidan mentioned that the two of you have decided to not see each other anymore." Amelia's eyes drilled into Maura's face.

Maura nodded. "Things just didn't work out between the two of us." She stared out the window at the manicured green lawn. "Maybe I shouldn't have come here today."

"Oh, no. I'm glad you're here. I really appreciate your help. Whatever happened between you and Aidan is your own business. Although, I must say that I thought the two of you were good for each other. I hadn't seen Aidan that happy in a long time."

A tear sprang to Maura's eye. She hadn't been that happy in a long time either. "It just didn't work out. We wanted different things," she said softly. That was a major under-statement, but it was the closest thing to the truth that she felt like telling his sister.

Amelia stood and walked over to Maura, bending down to hug her. "I'm sorry it didn't go better. If you ever want to talk about it, let me know."

Maura nodded. Amelia was nice, and she'd come to think of her as a friend, but the idea of confiding in her ex's sister felt odd.

Amelia's manner turned businesslike. "Let me show you what I've decided on. If you think the furnishings don't seem appropriate to the early 1900s, let me know." She pulled out her laptop and clicked on a few things, before putting it on the coffee table and turning it to face Maura. She crouched down next to the table, pointing out items on the screen. "I have this pattern for the drapes, this for the rugs, and this for the rest of the furnishings for the guest rooms."

Maura peered at each picture, drinking in the details. Amelia had outdone herself. "I can't see anything wrong with these. I think they will be lovely together." She pictured the guest rooms with new decor. "I can't wait to see the final result."

Amelia beamed. "Me too." She gently shut the lid of the laptop. "I think we should be able to finish it by summer."

"That's great," Maura said, genuinely meaning it. She wanted the hotel to succeed, even if it would be under different management by then. "Do the new owners still plan to open by June?"

Amelia cocked her head to the side. "The new owners? Do you mean Aidan and me?"

"No, I mean the people that you're selling the hotel to."

Amelia's eyes widened. "We haven't made any decisions about selling the hotel yet. It's something we're considering, but we want to explore all of our options first." She looked more closely at Maura. "Why, did Aidan tell you we were selling?"

Maura squirmed a little in her seat. "Well, no, but he mentioned you'd received some offers."

Amelia's face was sober. "That's true. We have received

some good offers. Honestly, it's been much more expensive to renovate the hotel than we'd originally projected. Even with careful budgeting, we're nearing the end of our financial means. Aidan is stressed beyond words about it. Owning a hotel of our own has been a dream for years, and now that's in jeopardy." She pressed her lips together. "I think we'll figure out a way to make it work though."

Maura stared at Amelia. She hadn't realized that Aidan was under so much pressure. She should have known though – the way he'd blown up at her when she'd mentioned him selling the hotel had been uncharacteristic for him. Had she been unnecessarily cruel to him? That hadn't been her intention – she'd only wanted for him to tell her the truth about selling the hotel.

"Was that the only reason you broke up with him?" Amelia asked. "I mean, you don't have to tell me why, but I can't help but wonder if there's anything I can do to make things better between the two of you."

Was there a chance that their relationship could be fixed? A memory from the night before came back to Maura – Aidan telling her that she was causing him stress and making a bad situation worse. She didn't want to be the cause of more problems for him. The hotel's issues were enough to deal with on their own.

And, if she was causing him that much stress, it was unlikely that he felt about her the same way she felt about him. Even if he was under that much pressure, he hadn't been completely honest with her about what was going on. He hadn't shared his problems with her, which was a huge red flag in her book.

Maybe things had moved too fast between them, but she hadn't been able to stop herself from falling in love with him. Apparently, he hadn't had the same issue regarding her. She bit her lip to keep from crying.

"Like I said, we just wanted different things. There isn't really anything you can do." Maura forced a smile. "But thank you for your concern. I've come to consider you a friend, and I hope that even though things didn't work out between Aidan and me, you and I will remain friends."

Amelia hugged her. "Of course. I feel the same way. It hasn't been easy, moving to a new place where I know next to no one. I appreciate the kindness you've shown me." She gestured to the door. "What do you think about heading out to grab a cup of coffee in town? I spend so much time here that I'd love to get out a little."

"Sure." Maura looked at her gratefully. She could use a distraction to keep from thinking about Aidan not reciprocating the way she felt about him. Plus, she needed to get away from the hotel before he returned. She didn't want to risk running into him before she'd managed to rebuild the protective shell she usually wore to keep herself from getting hurt.

18

Aidan sat at the desk in the lobby on Wednesday night, running the numbers on the hotel for what seemed like the fiftieth time. Still not enough, no matter what he did to cut costs. There wasn't any way he and Amelia could afford to keep the hotel. They'd have to sell. He rested his forehead on the desk.

"Hey, buddy." Amelia came in and rested her hand on his shoulder. "I was thinking about going into town to get some Chinese food for dinner. Do you want to come too?"

He sighed and lifted his head to look at her. "Sure. Might as well. I can't seem to get our budget to magically balance."

"That bad?" She glanced at the notepad he'd scribbled all over, and scrunched up her nose. "I don't understand how you can make heads or tails out of that."

He gave her a weak smile. "Way too much practice." He stood from the desk and grabbed his coat off the back of his chair. "Are you ready to go?"

"Let me grab my purse and then I'll be ready." She returned a minute later, with her giant bag in hand. He always joked that she was ready for everything with that bag.

They got into his car and he pulled out of the parking lot.

"Has Maura called you back yet?" Amelia asked.

"Nope." He'd called her several times over the last few days and left messages, but she hadn't responded. He was starting to wonder if she ever would. He turned onto Main Street and parked in front of the Chinese restaurant.

After they were seated, they decided to share a family-style meal that turned out to be much more food than he'd expected.

"Yum." Amelia dipped a piece of barbecued pork into the spicy mustard. She looked up at him. "So, what are you going to do about Maura?"

"What do you mean?" His sister's nosiness held no bounds.

"How are you going to win her back?" Amelia asked. "I talked to her on Saturday and I could tell she was upset. She loves you."

"It doesn't seem that way. She hasn't called me back." The lo mein he'd eaten had turned into a ball of grease in his stomach.

"You hurt her," Amelia said patiently. "What do you expect?"

He slumped against the backrest of the red vinyl booth. "I didn't mean to. It's just I was so worried about the hotel, and everything I said to her came out wrong."

"Everyone makes mistakes, but if you don't talk to her, she'll never know how you feel." Amelia poured some sugar into her tea, blew on the top of it, and took a sip.

"She hates me." He sighed. "Not that it matters. We're not going to be here for much longer anyway since we have to sell the hotel. I feel like I'm failing on all counts."

She rubbed her finger along the edge of her porcelain tea cup. "What if we sell the house back in California?"

He looked up sharply. "What?"

"The last time I was down there, the renter mentioned again how much they'd like to purchase it. We could probably close on the sale fairly quickly."

"You'd want to do that?" He scanned her face. "You didn't want to sell Mom and Dad's house until we knew for sure that we were going to stay up here."

She shrugged. "You're happy here and have found a wonderful woman to love. The town is growing on me, and I love this hotel. I'd like to see what the future brings for us in Candle Beach."

He did some quick calculations in his head. With real estate prices the way they were in the Bay Area, they'd have no problem meeting all of their financial commitments if they sold the house. "Are you sure?" he asked again. "Once we make this decision, there's no going back."

"It's fine with me. Our new life is up here and I know Mom and Dad would be happy that their house was able to make our dreams for the future a reality." She studied him. "Should I call the renters and let them know we'll sell the house to them?"

A weight lifted from his chest and for the first time in a week, he felt like he could breathe. "Yes. Let them know."

She swallowed a bite of fried rice. "I'll call them tomorrow morning. Now that we have one problem solved, what are you going to do about Maura? It's a small town, and if we're staying here, that's going to be awfully hard for you to see her all the time."

His happiness deflated. "I don't know. If she won't return my phone calls, there's not much I can do."

She laughed and shook her head. "It's going to take more than a phone call. You need to let her know how much you love her. Think, bro. What would make her happy? Is there anything in particular that she's mentioned?"

He stared at the half-eaten food on the table. "She wants to find a location for the historical society's museum."

"Good. That's getting somewhere. Is there anything you can do about that?"

"She said there wasn't a space available anywhere in town that would work." What could he possibly do about that? He couldn't just make a space appear.

"What about the old barn? We don't really need it for anything at the hotel and I bet it would be about the right size. You had them fix it up a little, right?"

"Yeah." He pictured the barn. It was big and might be a little drafty, but it could work. Having the museum co-located with the hotel would be a win-win situation for attracting tourists to both. A slow smile slid across his face. "Amelia, you might be on to something."

19

Aidan rubbed his palms against his jeans, both to dry the clamminess from them and to stabilize himself. He had never felt more anxious, not even when big shots had stayed at the hotels he'd managed. This was more important than anything else he'd ever done in his entire life. Maura just had to like the surprise he'd prepared for her.

He hadn't been sure that she would come out to the hotel if he asked her, so he'd had Amelia invite her to come and see the finished hotel. They'd scrambled the last few weeks to pull off the final touches on the renovations, including his surprise for Maura, and they were ready for their grand re-opening event for the town the next weekend.

Maura wasn't due at the hotel for another fifteen minutes, but he felt as though he was about to jump out of his skin. He forced himself to walk slowly over to the edge of the cliff above the beach, taking in the sounds of nature as he walked. His head was oddly clear as he stood behind the freshly painted white fence, situated a secure three feet before the edge of the cliff. Seagulls screeched overhead, and the sun glinted off of the waves rushing in as high tide claimed its share of the sand.

His heart rate slowly returned to normal. These last three weeks without Maura had been one of the worst periods of his life that he'd ever experienced. He'd thrown himself into his work to the point where Amelia had urged him to slow down – but he hadn't been able to do so. After recommitting to the hotel project and knowing in his heart that Maura and Candle Beach were what he wanted, he wasn't going to stop until he'd given it his all. It had taken longer than he'd hoped to get the barn ready to show her, but he knew if he was going to win her back, it would take something big.

Soft steps padded through the short grass behind him.

"You okay?" Amelia shaded her eyes with her hand to block the sun, but he could still see the concern etched across her face.

He took a deep breath and smiled at her. Surprisingly, he *was* ready.

She lowered her arm to check her watch. "Maura should be here soon."

The butterflies returned and he glanced quickly out at the ocean to settle his nerves.

"I know." He shoved his hands in the pockets of the forest-green windbreaker he wore over his short-sleeve polo shirt, and walked toward his sister.

When he stood next to her, she put her hand on his arm and forced him to look at her directly.

"You're sure you're okay?" Her eyes searched his face.

"I'm as sure as I'm going to be."

She nodded sharply. "Okay then. Let's go."

They walked back to the hotel together.

Amelia paused inside the door to the lobby. "Do you want me to wait with you?"

"No. Thanks, but I need to do this myself."

She disappeared into the kitchen and he stared out through the crystal-clear glass of the new window in the lobby. Amelia had adorned it with a fabric made of blue swirls that replicated the colors of the ocean. He cast a quick glance around. Everything looked exactly as he'd planned. The floors shone with polish, and the wood of the front desk had been restored to its original condition. As far as he could tell, they hadn't missed a beat. Only time would tell how customers would react. But first, Maura would be the test. Where was she?

Gravel crunched in the parking lot and he stepped behind the desk.

A few minutes later, Maura pushed open the door. Immediately, her eyes met his.

"Oh," she said quietly. "I was expecting to see Amelia."

"I know." He came around to the front of the desk and stood about two feet from her. He wanted to be closer, but she likely needed her space.

She looked up at him. "Is she here?"

"She's here, but I had her invite you over because I was hoping to talk with you." He reached forward to lightly touch her arm. She didn't move away. "Is that okay with you?"

Her lips quivered, but she nodded.

Relief spread through his body, lightening his mood. "Thank you. I appreciate it. I feel things ended so suddenly between us before that we didn't have much of a chance to talk about it." He motioned to the room. "What do you think?"

She surveyed the lobby, and he followed her gaze. A small seating area with a formal but comfortable couch and chair bordered a dark oak coffee table. Amelia had artfully arranged a vase full of freshly cut roses and set them on another small table against the wall.

"It's beautiful." She ran her hand along the edge of the front desk and her gaze flickered to him. "You've done a wonderful job with it."

He smiled. "Thank you. That means a lot." He gestured to the door. "Would you like to see some of the grounds?"

She tilted her head up at him. "The grounds?"

"Yep." He held out his hand. She eyed it for what seemed like minutes, but was probably only a few seconds, then her warm hand curved around his. He grasped it and the nerves in his hand and arm lit up with happiness. This was the reaction he'd been hoping for. He squeezed her hand lightly and led her out of the hotel. She followed him to the garden he'd made along the back of the barn.

Her eyes widened. "Are those the tulips we bought in Willa Bay?"

"They are." He squeezed her hand again. "Well, some of them are from our trip to Willa Bay. I supplemented those with a few other varieties that bloom late in the year, but the rest of them I'll plant here this fall to bloom next spring."

"It's lovely." Her eyes were glued to the flowers. "I didn't know you were planning on putting in a formal garden here."

He shrugged. "I hadn't been." He tugged lightly on her hand to swivel her around to face him. "But someone close to me convinced me that we needed more flowers around here."

Her eyes sparkled and she threw her arms around his neck.

"I was hoping you'd come around. After seeing the gardens at the Willa Bay Lodge, I knew the Candle Beach Hotel needed some too." He started to reach for her waist, but she dropped her hands away from his neck and stepped back, as if unsure.

"I'm sorry. I shouldn't have done that," she whispered.

He sighed. "I'm glad you did though." He placed his hands on her shoulders. "Maura, I've missed you so much. I know I did some things that you found hurtful and I never meant for that to happen. I would give anything to take that back." He ran his hands down her arms.

"Me too." Her eyes sparkled with unshed tears. "I've been stressed about finding a place for the historical society's museum and I was upset about the possibility of you selling the hotel to some big company that only cared about profits." In a small voice, she added, "And it felt like you didn't care about me because you wanted to leave me and Candle Beach."

He vigorously moved his head from side to side. "No. I never wanted to leave you – or Candle Beach for that matter. For a while though, I thought selling the hotel was my only chance." He leaned against the side of the barn. "Everything was crashing down on Amelia and me and then those offers to buy the hotel came in, like they were there to save the day."

"What changed your mind?" she asked.

"You. I knew this was where my future was – here with you in Candle Beach."

"But where did you find the money?"

He glanced up at the brilliant blue sky, unmarred by even a marshmallow cloud. "We sold our parents' house back in the Bay Area."

She gasped. "But you wanted to keep it, just in case."

He shrugged again. "Amelia and I both realized that we needed to move on. If we were going to make a success of this place, we had to fully commit."

"That must have been difficult for you." She twisted her fingers. "I know how much it meant to you."

"Selling it wasn't as emotionally difficult as we'd thought." He laughed. "I guess Candle Beach had already grown on us."

She laughed too. "It has a tendency to do that." Then she sobered. "But what does that mean for us, now that you're staying here? The way I treated you when I was hurting, I didn't think there was any hope for a future together."

"I think that's what made me realize how much it meant to me to stay here and go all in with the hotel. You telling me how you felt was a wake-up call for me."

She rubbed her thumb against the top of his hand. "Do you think you can forgive me?"

He held his pointer finger up in the air. "Hold that thought."

Her mouth flapped open, but she didn't say anything as he led her around to the front of the barn.

He slid the bar lock back and flung open the doors. The sunlight lit up the front of the barn, but he strode ahead and flipped on a light, illuminating the rest of the space. The inside had received a full remodel, with smaller rooms created by blocking off some of the space on one side of the big open space. Just inside the door, a tall counter had been set up.

She looked around with a puzzled expression on her face. "I don't understand. I thought you were planning on tearing the barn down.

He grinned and turned around a large wooden sign that was propped against the desk, revealing the words *Candle Beach Historical Museum*. "That was the original plan – until a beautiful woman came into my life and brought to my attention the need for a museum in Candle Beach. This seemed like the perfect location for one."

Her eyes darted around the room and a wide smile spread across her face. "This is wonderful." She practically skipped across the floor, dancing in and out of the smaller rooms. She returned and threw her arms around him, tears streaming down her face. "I love it."

He pulled her close, resting his chin on the top of her head.

She looked up and dried her cheeks with the back of her hand, but her eyes still sparkled with happiness. "I can't believe you did all of this. It's more than I could have ever hoped for."

He leaned down and kissed her on the lips. She sighed contentedly and snaked her arms around his neck. He threaded his fingers through her hair and kissed her until they were both out of breath. When they came up for air, tears slipped out of her eyes.

He froze. "Is something wrong?"

"No, no." She laughed. "I'm just so happy." She paused. "But I don't know how the historical society will be able to afford the space." She gave him a wry grin. "We're not exactly rolling in dough. But I'll find a way. There's no way I'm losing out on the Candle Beach Hotel again."

He smoothed her hair back from her face, brushing a tear away with his thumb at the same time. "I've already arranged it with Agnes at the historical society. You'll be able to lease it for a dollar a month for the next fifty years."

"Really?" Her voice was giddy with delight. "You'd do that for the historical society? For me?"

She wasn't getting it. "Honey," he said. "I'd do anything for you. Plus, I intend to live in Candle Beach for the rest of my life, so it's in my best interest to help preserve its heritage." He laughed. "And it will be a nice tourist draw for the hotel."

She stood on her tiptoes to pull his head down to her,

kissing him so firmly on the lips that his insides seemed to turn molten.

"Wow," he said when she released him. "If I'd known that was the reward, I would have given you the hotel as soon as I met you."

She giggled and slugged him lightly on the arm. "You'll probably regret your offer to lease us the barn after I show you everything that needs to be moved into the space, but I'm not letting you go back on your offer."

"I wouldn't dream of it." He kissed her cheek and hugged her to his side. "This was the right thing to do."

She melted into him and they stood like that for a minute, taking in the future site of the Candle Beach Historical Museum.

When they left the barn, hand in hand, Maura felt as though she were walking on air. She'd come to the hotel that afternoon at Amelia's request, expecting to see the hotel in its finished state before it opened to the public. What she'd gotten instead was so much more.

She looked up at Aidan's handsome face, savoring the familiar feeling of his hand in hers. A breeze swept across the garden, causing the tulips and roses to flutter, but she barely felt its chill. She'd missed him so much, but she'd thought she'd ruined any chance for a relationship with him. She felt his eyes on her and he bent down to kiss the top of her head, warming her even more. They rounded the corner of the barn and walked toward the hotel together.

Amelia must have heard them, because she came bounding out the front door.

When she saw them holding hands, she clasped her

hands together, and her face lit up. "Yay!" she cried out. "I'm so happy you guys worked it out."

Heat rose in Maura's cheeks, but her thoughts echoed Amelia's sentiments.

"How did you like the museum building?" Amelia asked, bouncing up and down on the balls of her feet.

"It's wonderful," Maura said. "The other ladies at the historical society are going to love it."

"Oh, some of them have already seen it." Amelia leaned against a post on the front porch. "Agnes wanted to see it before she signed the lease."

Maura looked from sister to brother, unsure of how she felt about not being first to see the renovated barn. "They already know about it?"

Aidan smiled. "I wanted to get it cleared by them before I presented it to you. I didn't want to disappoint you again." He shook his head. "That Agnes drives a tough bargain."

Laughter burbled out of Maura's mouth. She couldn't be mad about them telling Agnes first. "That she does."

"Do you think we can get the museum set up in time for the grand opening of the hotel?" Amelia nodded at the barn. "We're planning on doing an outdoor barbecue for everyone in town for our soft opening next week. It would be nice to have them open at the same time."

Anxiety filled Maura's chest, but she pushed it down. Getting things ready in a week was a tall order, but she knew with Aidan's support, she could accomplish anything.

"I think it's definitely doable."

"Fantastic." Amelia beamed. "This is going to be an awesome grand opening. I can't wait."

20

Maura watched as Maggie opened up the pink onesie from Sarah.

"It's so cute." Delight crossed Maggie's face as she held it up to show everyone. "I can't wait until I can put it on her."

The other women squealed as they passed it amongst themselves. When it reached Maggie's mother, she folded it and stacked it with the other items her daughter had received.

Maura fought to hide a grin. Baby showers tended to be silly, but she was happy to be sharing this moment with Maggie, Dahlia, and their friends and family. For many of the years that she'd lived in Candle Beach, she hadn't had many friends. It hadn't seemed like a big deal until Sarah had introduced her to her own group of friends and Maura realized what she'd been missing. Now, she felt like she belonged in town.

And now with Aidan in her life, the feeling was even stronger. A delicious warmth spread throughout her body, and the noise of the shower-goers faded away. Aidan was everything she'd ever hoped to find in a man – someone who challenged her, but made her feel safe and loved at the same time. The grand opening of the hotel was next week-end, and she was excited to see what the future brought for them.

A sharp elbow to the stomach broke her away from her daydream.

"Ouch!" she cried out.

Gretchen held up a baby blanket in front of her, and Maura took it automatically before passing it on to the person next to her.

"Where were you?" Gretchen's eyes twinkled. "You looked like you were a million miles away."

Heat rose up Maura's cheeks. "I was thinking about the grand opening of the Candle Beach Hotel and Museum." She doubted Gretchen would buy it, but in her defense, her statement was partially true.

"Uh-huh." Gretchen snickered under her breath, then whispered, "And maybe thinking of a certain hotel owner?"

Maura elbowed her in return and shot her a withering look. Gretchen smirked, but quieted. They played some baby shower games, which didn't turn out as badly as Maura had feared. Everyone howled with delight when Dahlia's mother-in-law, Wendy, chose a string that was twice as wide as Dahlia's belly.

"Hey!" Dahlia protested as she grabbed the string and stared at it incredulously. "I'm not an elephant."

"Maybe there are twins in there." Wendy didn't look like she'd mind that at all.

"There aren't." Dahlia mock-glared at her and then gave her a hug.

"Eh, there's always next time." Wendy grinned mischievously. "Now that I've settled in one place, I can't think of anything I'd rather have than a bunch of little ones running around."

Dahlia patted her belly. "We're going to see how this one

goes before we start on a baseball team." She shook her head. "It's a tad bit terrifying to think I'll have a little person to care for in only a month. The last couple of months have gone by fast."

Maggie leaned over and hugged her, their swollen bellies touching each other. "Don't worry. You're going to be an awesome mom. And our babies will be friends forever, just like us."

Dahlia smiled and leaned into Maggie. Maura's stomach twinged. Like Dahlia had said, the thought of having her own baby was scary. Before she could stop the thought, she found herself thinking about what Aidan would be like as a father. It may have been a premature question, but she knew the answer – he would be wonderful.

She could already see their kids running across the lawn at the hotel, playing catch with Aidan as Barker ran between them, yelping his little head off. A few months ago, she'd been single and now she was imagining an entire future with someone. How quickly life changed. She let the thought linger in her mind, but turned part of her attention back to the shower.

After the gifts had been opened, Dahlia and Maggie remained in the living room to chat with their family members while the guests chose from Angel's signature cakes and pastries that Sarah had set up on the dining room table. Maura, Angel, Gretchen, Sarah and Charlotte gathered around the kitchen table to eat their desserts.

"I love how the remodel turned out," Angel said, looking around the kitchen. "I hope when Adam and I get married that we can find someplace like this."

"Married?" Gretchen asked. "Did Adam propose?"

Angel laughed. "No, not yet. But we've been talking about it." A dreamy look came over her face. "We've discussed a late summer wedding."

"Another wedding!" Charlotte said. "I love this. Weddings always make me so happy."

"Me too. I'm happy for you guys," Sarah said to Angel. "I think it will be a while before Patrick and I get there because we haven't had much time together yet, but I'm happy with how things are going between us." She smiled at Angel. "I'm glad you like the kitchen. We put a lot of effort into it."

Maura admired the gray granite countertops and white cabinets, accented by crystal door pulls. Sarah and Patrick had managed to keep the vintage look of the kitchen, but update it at the same time.

She dug into the large slice of fudge cake she'd placed on her plate. Lunch had gone by the wayside because she'd been too busy with Aidan, moving artifacts into the new museum, and now she was starving. She stretched her arms reflexively at the thought of all of those boxes they'd moved. Tomorrow, her muscles would be screaming.

She eyed her plate of chocolate cake and broke off another piece with her fork. At least she could justify the calories she was consuming – not that it would have stopped her from eating it anyway. Angel's cakes were not to be missed.

When she looked up, she noticed the other women's eyes on her. She'd heard them chattering, but she'd been focusing on the cake. What had she missed?

"What?" She wiped her mouth with the corner of a pink napkin, then took a sip of coffee.

Charlotte laughed. "Oh, nothing. We were just wondering when you were going to tell us about Aidan."

Maura almost choked on her coffee. Sputtering, she set the cup down on the table. Having close girlfriends was going to take some getting used to.

"Yeah. Why don't you tell us about Aidan?" Angel's eyes

danced as she bit into a piece of fluffy vanilla cake topped with yellow frosting.

Maura sighed, but she couldn't keep her lips from spreading into a huge smile. "He's decided to stay in Candle Beach – and we're back together."

Charlotte cheered. "That's so exciting."

"I'm happy for you," Angel said. "He seems like a really great guy."

"And that's not all," Sarah piped up. "He turned the old barn on the hotel property into a museum for the Candle Beach Historical Society."

Maura's pulse quickened, thinking of Aidan's joy as he surprised her with the new museum building. She really had gotten a good guy.

"Wow." Gretchen eyed her. "I figured he and Amelia would tear that down. It was pretty ramshackle back when we'd go out there as kids. That's fantastic that they were able to save it."

"It is. I still can't really believe we'll have all that space and so many people will get to learn about Candle Beach's history." Maura's heart filled with happiness.

"Now that the renovations are done, I can't wait to get out there to paint it," Charlotte said. "I painted it last year, but I think a before and after display would be fun. And I bet it will be popular with hotel guests when they see it at the art gallery where I sell my paintings."

"You know," Maura said, tapping her chin with her index finger. "I bet Aidan's sister Amelia would love to display some of your paintings in the hotel. She mentioned wanting to find some artwork for the upstairs hallways. You could probably loan her some on consignment."

Charlotte's face lit up. "Really? That would be great. Can you please introduce me to her?"

"No problem." Maura grinned. "Are you going to the grand opening next week?"

"I wouldn't miss it." Charlotte pulled out her phone and made a few notes. "I'll make sure to bring some examples of my art to show her. Thanks, Maura."

"You're welcome." It felt good to be able to help her friends, and she knew they'd do the same for her. A thought occurred to her. "By the way, would any of you be interested in helping me move some of the historical society's collections that are in storage into the museum this evening? Some of the other ladies from the society will be setting up the displays this week, but most of the women are elderly and it's difficult for them to carry the boxes from the hotel's parking lot."

"Sure. I can come over after the shower," Charlotte said.

"Me too," Gretchen added.

Angel and Sarah nodded in agreement.

"I'd love to see the space," Angel said. "It looks like the party is winding down. Maybe we can get Sarah's house cleaned up and then head over to the storage facility to grab some stuff?"

"Sounds good to me." Maura beamed. She'd thought she'd be working all night at the museum, because Aidan had some things to do for the hotel's grand opening and wouldn't be able to assist her any more that day. "Thank you all for your help."

They rejoined Dahlia, Maggie and the others in the living room to continue celebrating the two new babies that would soon be a big part of their friends' lives.

CHAPTER 21 AND AUTHOR'S NOTE

The townspeople had started to arrive a little before noon for the grand opening of the Candle Beach Hotel, and Aidan wondered if his stomach would ever return to normal. It had been a mass of nerves since he'd woken up, a little after sunrise. This was the day he'd show the hotel to everyone and find out what they thought of his and Amelia's renovation.

They'd lucked out, and Mother Nature had smiled down on them with a day filled with sunshine, blue skies, and high clouds that were fluffy enough to put unsheared sheep to shame. Maura had helped him and Amelia put the finishing touches on the property, and although there would always be more to do, he couldn't think of anything at the moment that could make things more perfect. They'd hired the Bluebonnet Café to cater the event and had invited everyone in town to attend. The first overnight guest would arrive in a week, but this event was just to show the locals the renovated property and celebrate with them.

Luke and Charlotte were two of the first people to arrive. They held hands, swinging them effortlessly between their bodies as they walked across the grass to where he stood by the deck stairs. For the event, he and Amelia had hung red and blue balloons from the deck supports and several signs around the property reading *Candle Beach Hotel – Grand Re-Opening.* As he leaned against one of the balloons, it squeaked under his weight, and he stepped forward to keep it from popping.

"Aidan, buddy. This place looks awesome." Luke reached out to Aidan and shook his hand. "I love that porch. I could sit there in one of those Adirondack chairs for hours, just drinking a beer and relaxing."

Aidan's chest swelled with pride. "That's the idea. We want our guests to feel comfortable here and enjoy the magic of being at the ocean."

"You've done a wonderful job. That turret with the widow's walk is like a topper on a beautiful cake." Charlotte scanned the hotel from top to bottom. "Maura has been telling us about all of the renovations, but it's exciting to see them in person. Is she around?"

Aidan pointed at the barn, across the grass lawn. "She's over at the new historical museum. She and the other members are all taking shifts there." He checked his watch. "Her shift should be done soon."

"We'll head over and say hi to her then," Charlotte said. "I'm sure you have lots of people to greet today."

Aidan smiled at her. "I'm never too busy for my friends." He clapped Luke on the back. "Besides, without this guy, I wouldn't be standing here."

Luke grinned. "True. Nevertheless, we'll head over to the barn and leave you to greet your adoring guests." He shook his head. "I would never have believed how beautiful this place could look."

"Thanks," Amelia said, coming up behind him, wearing a sundress he knew she'd bought for the occasion, because she'd tortured him for hours with questions about which dress looked best.

He introduced his friends to his sister.

"Say, you're Charlotte, Maura's friend, right?" Amelia asked.

"I am." Charlotte laughed. "Why, what has she said about me?"

"Only that you're the most talented artist on the planet," Amelia said. "She mentioned you might be interested in showing some of your artwork at the hotel to sell on a consignment basis."

Charlotte's eyes widened. "She did?"

"Yep. And I think that's a fantastic idea." Amelia pulled out her cell phone and handed it to Charlotte. "Give me your phone number and we can set up a time to go over things. I'd like to see your paintings first, and then we can decide what will best fit here. I'm sure our clientele will go nuts for local artwork though."

"Thanks. I'd love that." Charlotte typed her phone number into Amelia's cell phone. "That was nice of Maura to mention me."

"Nice for us." Amelia put the phone back in her pocket. "She's been a great resource over the last few months for local craftsmen in the area, and now she's hooked us up with some great artwork too. I don't know what we would do around here without her." She cast a sidelong glance at Aidan. "Good thing my brother didn't manage to chase her away permanently."

"Which time?" His lips twisted into a smile, thinking about the first time he'd met Maura, when he'd caught her trespassing in the hotel.

"Either," she joked back.

"Aidan!" a male voice called out. He turned to see Parker and Gretchen coming toward their little group.

"I love what you've done with this place." Gretchen pointed to the hotel. "I can't believe when we were kids, we thought it was haunted. I once won five bucks when Johnny Dobly bet me I wouldn't walk into the lobby alone."

"Ah, so you're one of the teen vandals we've heard so much about," Aidan teased.

Gretchen waved her hand in the air. "Nah, we never did anything like that. Although someone did. I couldn't believe what bad condition the hotel was in just a few months ago when we got the listing."

"No kidding." Amelia laughed. "When Aidan told me he wanted to buy the hotel, I did think he was a little out of his mind. He assured me that we could make it shine, but I had my doubts." She turned to him. "Big brother – this is me, officially admitting I was wrong."

He gasped and stepped back. "Did I really just hear my little sister admitting she was wrong about something?"

She stuck her tongue out at him. "You'll never hear it again, so enjoy it this one time."

"Oh, Amelia," Gretchen said. "Actually, Parker and I wanted to talk with you about something."

Amelia tipped her head to the side. "About what?"

"Maura reminded me that you're an interior designer and we're looking for some help with the properties Parker is renovating. Our friend Patrick is remodeling the buildings, but we need design consults for each house." She wrinkled her nose. "My sense of style isn't great and neither is Parker's. We don't want to accidentally do something that will turn off buyers, so we'd love your help."

Amelia's face lit up. "I'd love that. Give me a call when you're ready for me to help. Also, if you hear of any other design projects in the area, please let me know. Now that the hotel is mainly complete, I'll be looking for some interior design jobs to do when I'm not helping here."

"Sounds great." Gretchen sniffed the air. "Do I smell blueberry pie?"

"You do." Amelia turned and pointed toward the other side of the hotel. "The food is set up near the back deck, and it's delicious. You should grab some before they run out of the blueberry pie."

"Will do." Parker took Gretchen's hand, then waved at them with his other hand. "We'll catch up with you guys later, after we've been fed."

The others laughed and said goodbye. Aidan couldn't blame them for jetting away. He'd had some of the juicy fruit pie earlier and was contemplating another piece. When he'd called to place their catering order, Angel had told him it was one of their best sellers, and now he knew why.

"I'll take over here if you want to go with your friends to see Maura," Amelia said.

"Thanks. I'll check back in with you in a little bit, okay?"

"Aye, aye, captain." She mock saluted him, then moved to greet an older couple walking up the lawn toward them.

Luke, Charlotte, and Aidan walked over to the barn together. They were talking about something, but Aidan wasn't following their conversation. Amelia had been right. His life would have been extremely different without Maura in it. Without her, he may have given up on the hotel, and even if he'd still managed to succeed with it, his life would have been empty without her. That fateful phone call of Luke's had been a major catalyst for change in his life.

After the last party guest had gone home and the catering crew from the Bluebonnet Café had packed up their tent and supplies, Maura and Aidan collapsed onto the chairs on the front deck with Barker. Aidan had asked her if she wanted to bring her dog to the event, and she'd gone home after her shift at the museum to get him so he wouldn't be cooped up all day. Barker had found quite a fan base among the party guests, who'd thought he was the cutest thing they'd ever seen.

"Well, I'd say that was a success." Maura forced herself to relax. It had been a long, stressful day with the grand opening of both the hotel and the museum, but it had been worth it.

"No kidding, I think everyone in town was here today." A huge smile filled Aidan's face. "Now if it's only that popular with the out-of-town guests."

Maura looked up at him sharply. "Are you worried about not having enough guests? I thought it was fully booked for the next month."

He sighed. "It is. I just can't help worrying that it's some kind of fluke."

She rose from her chair and walked over to him, wrapping her arms around his shoulders from behind. "You and Amelia have done a wonderful job on the renovation. Once word gets out, I wouldn't be surprised if by the end of the week you're booked solid for the rest of the summer." She glanced around. "Where is Amelia anyway?"

"She went to her room as soon as the caterers left. She wants to get up early tomorrow to photograph the sunrise so she can put some photos of it up on our website." He reached up to grasp her arms, his touch causing her skin to tingle pleasantly as his hands moved upward. He turned to face her. "Do you want to check out the gazebo? I haven't been out there at night since we finished the remodel."

"Sure." She moved aside to allow him room to stand, grabbing Barker's leash.

He reached out for her free hand, encircling her fingers

with his comforting warmth. The weather had been nice earlier, in the high sixties, but the temperature had dropped as soon as the sun went down. She shivered as they walked toward the gazebo and he hugged her tightly against him.

"Cold?" he asked.

"A little." She pulled her light windbreaker closer to her body. "I think I'll be okay once we're in the gazebo and out of the wind." They walked quickly across the grass, with Barker trotting along beside them.

The fresh white paint on the gazebo shone in the moonlight, and the scent of the roses planted next to it danced in the air. They climbed the steps to enter the gazebo, gazing out on the moonlit beach below.

"Remember all those wedding photos from that album I found?" he asked. "Just think, all those happy couples were standing in front of the same gazebo we're in right now." His voice was full of wonder.

"It's like we're part of the hotel's history," she said. "I wonder if some of those couples are still around. If so, I bet they'd love to see the renovated hotel."

He turned to her and planted a kiss on the top of her head. "That's a great idea. I'll see if there are any names on the back of the photos. Maybe we can get in touch with some of them."

"I can ask Agnes and the other ladies at the historical society to take a look too. They should be able to identify some of the locals in those pictures." She turned to look back over the shadowy lawn, where most of the pictures had been taken. "Seriously, if these walls could talk, think of all the wonderful stories they could tell."

"I know." He reached for her and held her close as they contemplated their role in history. "Maybe someday we'll be standing in front of the gazebo, having our wedding picture taken."

She looked up sharply. "Our wedding picture?"

He grinned. "I kind of like the idea of it." Then he sobered. "We're both in our mid-thirties and not getting any younger. Honestly, I've never been much for dating."

She nodded. "Me neither."

"I hope I'm not scaring you off." He searched her face. "All I mean is that I'm serious about you, Maura, and I know we have a future together."

"I think I like the sound of that too." She reached her hand up to stroke his cheek, and he lightly pressed his lips against hers. She closed her eyes and let the sensation of being close to him take over. This was what happiness felt like.

Author's Note

Thank you for reading Sweet Surprises. If this is your first Candle Beach Sweet Romance, check out the rest of the series to read about Maura's friends as they find love in unexpected places.

Candle Beach Sweet Romances
    Sweet Beginnings (Book 1)
    Sweet Success (Book 2)
    Sweet Promises (Book 3)
    Sweet Memories (Book 4)
    Sweet History (Book 5)
    Sweet Matchmaking (Book 6)

Jill Andrews Cozy Mysteries
    Brownie Points for Murder (Book 1)

ACKNOWLEDGMENTS

Thank you to my editors and cover designer for their help in making this the best book possible.

Editing: Serena Clarke, Free Bird Editing

LaVerne Clark, LaVerne Clark Editing

Cover Design: Mariah Sinclair